Salem Galdesque was busy doing a favor for one of Master Krispin's allies when the news of several beloveds in his home coven reaches his ears. He's happy for them even as he snickers at the shackles it places upon them. As his coven's fixer, he could only imagine the trouble such a bond would cause to his own life. Salem loves being able to solve a problem by any means necessary—whether it be by a payoff, seduction, or a good, old-fashioned beat-down . . . and maybe even more—and answering to a beloved would be nothing but a headache. His tactics makes his job easy, not to mention fun. When Salem is called home to the Maven coven, he meets the gargoyle Keefe and realizes Fate has bestowed upon him a rather dubious gift—Keefe is his beloved. After just a couple of encounters, Salem knows that between Keefe's serious need to color inside the lines and Salem's own prevalence toward shades of gray, their different outlooks will cause nothing but problems. Still, Keefe is Salem's beloved, and he knows he only gets one, so they come to an agreement—no talking shop with each other. When they both uncover leads regarding the hunters troubling the Maven coven, can they figure out how to work together, or will their issues tear not only them apart, but the coven as well?

The Fixer's Enforcer
Copyright © 2021 Charlie Richards
ISBN: 978-1-4874-3470-0
Cover art by Angela Waters

Published by eXtasy Books Inc

Look for us online at:
www.eXtasybooks.com

The Fixer's Enforcer
A Paranormal's Love: Book Thirty-Five

By

Charlie Richards

CHAPTER ONE

Creeping through the shadows, Salem Galdesque tailed his mark. He watched the rogue vampire pause and peer over his shoulder. The man obviously missed him, for he continued on at a relaxed pace. When he reached a non-descript door in the side of a run-down warehouse, he went inside.

Ah, so that's where you're hiding them.

Salem had been tailing James for two days—one of six rogues making up the gang—waiting for him to lead him to the missing men and women. While he was actually a member of the Maven coven in Wyoming, the leader there—Master Krispin Stearling—often loaned him to other covens that required his special brand of expertise. In this case, a small vampire coven in upstate New York just wasn't equipped to deal with a team of rogue vampires kidnapping people.

When Salem reached the door, he pressed his ear to the wall. As a vampire with exceptional hearing, he made out the sound of James hollering, "Where are Glade and Winston?"

"They're still out collecting," Salem heard another man answer.

"Still?" James growled, not sounding at all pleased. "They were supposed to be back half an hour ago. Our buyers will be here in twenty, and we're short their two."

Oh, now this is absolutely perfect.

Salem grinned broadly. If there were two vampire rogues still out, that meant there could possibly be only four inside the warehouse.

Not only will I be able to snag the whole gang, but I'll get a bead on their buyers, too.

Pulling out his phone, Salem sent off a quick text to Esposito and Illard, ordering them to meet him at the warehouse's address *ASAP*. He tucked his phone away, then peered down the alley, up at the building, and over at the one beside it. Spotting a fire escape on the nearby building and several broken third-story windows on the one the rogue had entered, Salem grunted with pleasure.

Salem moved to the fire escape, crouched for a second, gauging where the ladder hung overhead. Then he lunged upward. With his vampire strength and agility—plus his height advantage at being six-foot-five—he easily reached it. In near silence, Salem climbed to the roof of the building.

Standing at the edge, Salem judged the distance. He took a few steps backward, then sprinted forward. Planting his right foot on the ledge, he jumped, easily clearing the space between the buildings.

Outstretching his hands, Salem grew his claws ... and sank them into the wood frame of one of the broken window panes. He hung there for a few seconds, allowing the momentum to leave his body. After a glance around, Salem stretched out his leg and found purchase on the right side of the frame. There was nothing on the left, but he didn't need it.

With a careful push off the frame, a twist of his body, and the flex of his biceps, Salem swung onto the framework making up the wooden balcony. Unfortunately, it was a very old wooden balcony. A board creaked under his weight, and dust and debris clattered onto the floor below.

"What was that?" James demanded.

Salem crouched and stared between a gap in the slats, trying to take in the lay of the land. There was plenty of dust, broken machines of a use which Salem couldn't determine, and ... three vampires standing near an area that had been set up as a crappy living room—complete with dirty sofas, scuffed coffee tables littered with pizza boxes and beer bottles, and a very pale, slender young woman reclining on the sofa with blood dripping down her neck.

Considering how the female's eyes were closed and the shallow rise and fall of her breasts, Salem knew she was alive. He had every intention of keeping her that way. That meant taking out the trash.

And figuring out where the fourth rogue is hiding before his pals arrive.

"I don't know," the blond vampire answered with a dismissive shrug. "Probably a wild animal or somethin'."

James glared at him. "Well, go check it out, Vic," he snapped, slapping him upside the head.

Vic curled his lip and snarled, but he did as James had ordered, stalking toward a rickety-looking set of stairs to the left. He even grumbled under his breath as he focused his attention on deciding where to put each step. James didn't blame him, considering he felt the tremors shiver through the framework with each of the man's steps.

Still, it did give Salem the opportunity he needed. Grabbing the banister in one hand, he swung over the railing. He lifted his knees, let go, and rotated as he fell. Stretching out his right arm, Salem caught himself on a pole beam at second-story height and swung around it. He released it just as he heard James shout, but he ignored the vampire.

Salem focused on his target, instead—the black-haired rogue standing next to James. As he landed beside the man, he whipped out his hand, his claws extended. Even before the wet thud of the bleeding head hit the floor, Salem was turning toward James.

Blocking James's slashing strike with his own claws, Salem slammed the talons of his right hand deep between the ribs of the rogue leader. "Where's your friends, James?" he taunted as he yanked his claws back out and took a step away.

Salem spotted James's snarl as the rogue swung at him

once again. That time, he jumped backward to avoid the strike . . . having seen Vic leaping at him from overhead. Spinning and leaping, Salem hook-kicked Vic across his face, sending him crashing into James.

Both vampires went flying, bodies landing with sharp thuds and limbs sprawling.

Gods, it's like shooting fish in a barrel.

Jumping close, Salem had Vic's head lopped off before he'd even gotten his bearings. He'd intended to play with James a little longer—just for fun . . . and information—when the squeak of a door to his left drew his attention. A heavy-lidded vampire appeared from within the room.

"What's going on?" he slurred as if drunk . . . or blood-engorged.

Bastard.

In short order, Salem decapitated James before jumping on the moronic rogue. The dark-haired guy had barely even registered him, his eyes widening in surprise, before Salem removed his head from his shoulders. As the body fell, he rested his hands on his hips and peered around.

"Well," Salem grumbled. "That was just too damn easy."

A whimper caught his attention.

Taking three steps, Salem reached the doorway. He barely suppressed an angry growl as he surveyed the dirty space. Four humans—two men and two women, all appearing in their early twenties—sat on dirty mattresses, their hands and feet trussed before them. A fifth human—a male—lay unconscious on another mattress. Similar to the unconscious woman in the other room, blood dribbled from a pair of fang holes in his neck.

Gods, they couldn't even be bothered to close their damn bites.

The stench of fear permeated the room.

Doing his best to school his expression into something that resembled reassurance—not something Salem knew his hard features were good at—he lifted his hands in placation. "Everything is going to be all right," he rumbled.

When the stink of fear increased, coupled with gasps and cringes, Salem spotted what they were staring at. He still had his claws out. They were also covered in the blood of the rogues.

Just great. Where's Esposito when I need him?

The other vampire appeared of Mexican descent, and while he was still a badass enforcer, he could easily charm just about any human.

Salem heard the sound of a lock unbolting so he turned away from the frightened humans. Sprinting toward the opening warehouse door, he watched two vampires enter. Each carried a human—one male and one female—and both were unconscious.

Thank the gods for small favors.

The pair's expressions had just morphed into shock at seeing their fallen comrades when Salem reached them. He wasted no time in grabbing the female from the startled vampire. At the same time, Salem slashed his talons through his neck, taking him out.

Salem spun to face the final rogue. Keeping his focus on the blond, he slowly knelt and placed the human on the dirty floor. As he rose to his feet, Salem offered the man a feral grin.

"So, you ready to die like the rest of your friends?" Salem asked gruffly, taking a slow step toward the vampire, gauging the best way to get the human to safety before killing the male.

The vampire sneered. "Not friends." He chuckled coldly. "And with them out of the way, I'll get all the profit." With a cocky grin, he tossed the young man onto a nearby sofa. "I bet you beat the others due to the element of surprise. Won't happen with me."

Salem swept his gaze over the cocky vampire. Considering he seemed to like to talk, he couldn't help but ask, "So, this is your operation?" He grinned as he needled, "I thought James was the boss."

Curling his lip, the blond vampire narrowed his eyes. "You thought wrong," he declared, his fingers curling and uncurling, betraying his rising agitation. "I was just biding my time before taking over, letting him do all the work."

Then the blond lunged.

While Salem was tempted to play with the vampire, the stirring of one of the humans on the sofas changed his mind. The woman didn't deserve to wake up to this asshole's ranting. With that in mind, Salem dispatched him quickly with a spin and swipe.

Salem bent over and tore off the back of the downed vampire's shirt. Swiftly, he cleaned the blood from his talons before retracting them. Then he tossed the soiled fabric onto the blond's bare back.

"Well, fuck, Salem. Didn't you leave any fun for us?"

Grinning, Salem turned to face Illard and spotted Esposito standing beside him. Illard was leaning against the door frame, a smirk curving his dark lips. Esposito was peering around the warehouse, concern filling his expression when his attention fell on the humans.

"Sure, I left you some fun, Illard," Salem replied with a smirk. "Their buyers are supposed to show in just a few minutes. We can take them down, too."

Illard grinned broadly. "Sweet."

"This one's coming around," Esposito called, crouching beside the sofa. "Maybe clear those bodies away so she doesn't have to see them." Grimacing, he added, "Not that we can do anything about the blood spatter."

Salem shrugged, unrepentant. "Maybe she'd appreciate seeing proof that her attacker is dead." Even as he said the words, he grabbed a severed head by its hair as well as the leg of one of the bodies. "Oh, and there's five more humans in the storage room over there." Salem used his chin to indicate direction.

"Damn," Esposito grumbled. "Eight missings. Six rogues." He licked his forefingers before sliding them across the woman's puncture wounds, which had been left by one of the rogues' fangs. Using his saliva to seal them, Esposito removed the evidence of the vampire's bite. "No wonder the local coven asked for aid."

As Salem dragged the body, carrying the head, he grinned broadly. "Happy to help."

Taking his burden behind some rusting machine that had been left behind probably almost a century before, Salem left them there. He headed to the next body. Just as he grabbed a leg, he felt his phone vibrate within his pocket. As Salem pulled it free, he started toward the corner.

"Salem," he answered without checking the screen. There were very few who would call him. He noticed Illard had crossed to the storage room and was speaking in low tones while Esposito continued to help the three in the main room — the other vampire had even moved the woman Salem had placed on the floor to another of the sofas.

"Salem, how's your task going there?"

Hearing Master Krispin's voice, Salem returned his attention to his call as he continued moving bodies. Not only did Esposito's idea probably have merit, but he also wanted them out of the way for when the slavers arrived, too.

"We've located and eradicated the rogues here," Salem began. "Hopefully, we'll be able to start clean-up soon."

"Hopefully?" Master Krispin clearly wanted an explanation.

"Yes, Master," Salem replied formally. "They were holding six humans on the premises, and the final pair of rogues to show up were bringing two more." Before his master could voice anything, Salem quickly added, "Before taking them out, I overheard the head rogue say that their buyers were supposed to arrive soon."

"Damn," Master Krispin grumbled. "Bastards selling humans." His tone took on a musing quality. "Were they selling them to other vampires or humans?"

"Unknown at this time, Master," Salem admitted. He hadn't even considered that. "Illard and Esposito are checking the humans while I'm clearing bodies, and we're waiting for the buyers."

Master Krispin hummed for a few seconds. "Have you notified Master Levonne that you'll need an assist to aid those humans, yet?"

Salem frowned. "Not yet. We'd just finished killing the rogues when you called."

Chuckling, Master Krispin questioned, "We? Or you?"

Scoffing, Salem smirked. His master knew him so well. "Me. I couldn't wait for back-up, and there were only three in the room to start."

"Ah, so easy pickings," Master Krispin teased.

Salem grinned broadly. "Absolutely."

His amusement clear, Master Krispin continued, "Of course."

Hearing Master Krispin sound so relaxed still surprised Salem. The man's happiness managed to shine through the line in only a few words. While the master had never been a hard-ass, in the past, he'd always come across as business-like and unapproachable.

That had all changed when not only Master Krispin but several other people in the coven had found their beloveds — the other halves of their souls, promised by Fate. As odd as it seemed to Salem, they'd found their partners in gargoyles, of all things. The rumors were rampant in the coven in regards to who would find their beloved next.

Salem wished them all well, even as he felt grateful that he was out on assignment. While technically Salem's rank was that of an enforcer, everyone in his coven knew what he really was—a fixer. His master outlined a problem, and he solved it, by any means necessary.

Sometimes, that involved bribery. On occasion, Salem had enjoyed a night of seduction to get someone to do as the coven had needed. Mostly, however, his job involved what he was doing now . . . taking out the trash of their society.

Salem enjoyed it, too, and he couldn't imagine how some random person—beloved or not—could understand his job.

Just then, Salem noted the sound of an approaching vehicle. "I'm sorry, Master Krispin. I hear an approaching engine," he explained. "I'll need to call you back."

"When you do, tell me how swiftly you can get back here, even if Esposito and Illard need to stay," Master Krispin ordered. "I want you back asap."

Arching one brow, Salem froze. "You do?"

"I do." Master Krispin's tone hardened, all of his newly acquired relaxation and happiness disappearing. "We're dealing with priests."

"Fuck," Salem growled. "Understood."

Then Salem disconnected the call and prepared to finish his mission.

Chapter Two

Keefe woke slowly, the hold of roost releasing him. Staring up at the sky, he inhaled deeply before exhaling again. While the city lights managed to drown out most of the stars overhead, Keefe could still see a few.

In his mind, staring at the night sky was . . . peaceful. Everything was in its proper place. The placement of the stars was how people had managed to navigate the open seas for centuries.

Even though Keefe understood that suns could explode and stars could burn out, it wasn't until massive telescopes were invented that people had figured that out.

To Keefe, the night sky and the stars above were reliable.

Unlike people — human and paranormal alike.

And Fate.

Shaking his head, Keefe rose to his feet. He stretched his arms overhead and arched his back. Turning this way and that, he flared his wings and enjoyed the slight current across his sensitive appendages.

In the past, Keefe would have stepped to the edge of the building, snapped out his wings, and flown to the balcony of his assigned room.

Not anymore.

Keefe had become an enforcer for the gargoyle Circle of Elders almost two centuries before. To be entrusted with the safety of their kind's most esteemed leaders was a position of honor. He'd guarded the backs of just about everyone in the circle at one time or another.

And some I definitely like better than others.

To that end, when Keefe had landed as an enforcer for Elder Vermidian, he'd found the male honorable. While the man wasn't strict, he was ethical, always getting to the bottom of any problem he'd run across, and never taking one side over the other's until proof was found.

Admiring the male, Keefe had requested to become part of Vermidian's regular enforcer pool—each unmated gargoyle elder had four, normally a mixture of mated and unmated men, allowing them to keep him safe during all hours. The elder had lived in Ohio, but when he'd been tasked with an assignment taking him to Wyoming, he'd discovered his beloved in a vampire—Ridger Carruthers. The vampire had been the second of his coven, so Vermidian had uprooted his life and moved into not only the city, but the coven house—a high-rise hotel.

While Keefe missed the beauty of the stars, he tried to understand why Vermidian had done it. Supposedly, finding the other half of your soul was the greatest gift possible. From Keefe's observations, it also made people do some dumb shit.

Love is blind and all that.

Keefe still wanted to wring Vermidian's neck for accompanying his vampire mate into a dangerous situation, and that had been almost two weeks prior. The elder wasn't supposed to go rushing into danger. That was what his enforcers were for.

"Hey, Keefe. You gonna stand around stargazing all night?"

Turning, Keefe scowled at Phineas. The pale-brown gargoyle grinned broadly at him, amusement dancing in his dark eyes. The male was a fellow circle enforcer as well as the gargoyle he was mostly paired with unless either made a request for some reason. As much as they could rub each other wrong, like oil and water, Keefe still considered the fellow enforcer his friend.

"I was thinking about it," Keefe quipped back, a low growl in his tone. "The stars are so much more interesting than . . . you."

Phineas tipped his head back and laughed, his mouthful of sharp, white teeth gleaming in the moonlight. Not at all put off by Keefe's attitude—he never was—he patted him on the shoulder. Still smiling, Phineas turned toward a cabinet off to the side of the rooftop garden where they roosted each day.

At least we're not stuck inside.

Keefe followed Phineas to the cabinet and watched the other gargoyle open a drawer. After his friend pulled out his phone and wallet, Keefe did the same. Their actions were copied by the third unmated gargoyle in their unit—a new gargoyle enforcer arrival by the name of Perconz. So far, Keefe found him to be quiet and competent, doing what was needed with watchful efficiency.

The rooftop garden oasis had been created for the inner circle's use—more specifically, for vampire master Krispin Stearling. The man enjoyed relaxing with yoga—the cabinet proper contained a number of towels and yoga mats—but he hadn't wanted any but his closest friends to know. Hence, the private garden—the elevator to it stopped at only one floor, the thirteenth.

That floor contained the suites of the coven's three founding members—Master Krispin, Second Ridger, and Head Enforcer Basques. There was also those three's offices, and a large, private conference room. All three men were now mated. In fact, Krispin had recently given birth to his and his gargoyle beloved's first egg. The man's mate—the gargoyle Washington, Wash to his friends—just about bristled with pride whenever anyone questioned him about his eggling—Krispin's term for their unhatched son.

While Keefe knew that most gargoyles welcomed, even celebrated, the birth of any offspring, he had to hide an internal shudder each time he was faced with a wee one. Children, in general, were the opposite of orderly and predictable. Plus, they were messy as hell and often stinky.

Keefe prayed his own mate—should the Fates decide to bless him in such a manner—would not want kids. Cinnamon, a natural contraceptive to gargoyle sperm, was his best friend. It helped that he was more than happy to always bed men, although he hadn't been interested in any of the single vampires at the coven, and it wasn't as if he could seduce a human, considering most didn't even know of the existence of paranormals.

"So, tell me what's bothering you."

Hearing Phineas's demand pulled Keefe out of his thoughts. "What?"

Yep, that's an inane response.

Narrowing his eyes, Phineas stared at him even as he poked the down button. The elevator car opened to them swiftly enough. There was only one other stop, after all.

"What's on your mind?" Phineas pressed, leading the way into the car. "You haven't even called in yet this evening," he pointed out. "That's normally the first thing you do as soon as you pick up your phone."

Keefe grimaced as he rubbed the back of his neck. "Just worried about the elder," he admitted, before lifting his phone and calling Dennis, a gargoyle circle enforcer who'd arrived a few days before. As a mated gargoyle, Dennis could not only stay awake during daylight hours, but he also had a human form. That allowed him to guard the elder during the day, something vital now that Elder Vermidian also had a human form. When Dennis answered, Keefe commented gruffly, "Awake from roost. Heading down. Anything needing our immediate attention?"

Even as Keefe saw a grinning Phineas roll his eyes, Dennis responded as if by rote, "No, Enforcer Keefe. Nothing pressing. The standard hour of free time after roosting applies before a shift starts."

Keefe had heard that same reply each time he'd called Dennis. In truth, it was standard procedure. Upon waking from roost, an enforcer would have an hour of free time to clean up, relax, and eat a meal, before their shift began. That was on days Keefe worked, anyway.

Seeing as there were now four enforcers assigned to Vermidian, Keefe enjoyed one day off in seven. Due to having mated, Vermidian would be receiving another pair of enforcers—one mated and one not—bringing his total to six. They would be arriving within the week. Then each of them would have two days off in every seven.

Well, *enjoyed* was a relative term. He pretty much sat around in his suite and tried not to grow too bored. With the vampire coven living on the top floors of a high-rise hotel, it wasn't as if Keefe could go out and explore. He had no idea what he would do with himself with two days off.

Keeping the knowledge of paranormals secret from humans was the law of their world.

"Thank you," Keefe replied automatically.

Before Keefe could lower the phone and disconnect the call, Dennis continued, "Elder Vermidian wished me to inform you, Phineas, and Perconz that there's a mandatory meeting at nine in Master Krispin's conference room."

"Thank you," Keefe said again. On reflex, he added, "What's it about?"

"Master Krispin's fixer returned this morning," Dennis told him. "And he's already found something. He'll debrief us all at that time."

"Okay." Keefe glanced from Phineas, who furrowed his brow ridges, to Perconz, who just shrugged. "Who and what is a fixer?"

Keefe didn't get an answer, and he realized Dennis had already hung up. Sighing, he clipped his phone to one of the leather straps criss-crossing his chest. "Any ideas?" Keefe murmured as he pulled his hotel suite's keycard from his wallet.

"Maybe just how it sounds," Perconz guessed.

Phineas nodded, rubbing his chin. "A guy who fixes things . . . by any means necessary."

"Not a very flattering job description," Keefe commented as the elevator descended. "Sounds almost like a mobster or something."

Snorting, Phineas shook his head. "I think humans who hear the words *enforcer* and *second* probably immediately jump to thoughts of the mob, so why wouldn't a coven have a fixer, too?"

"Huh," Perconz muttered. "They do kinda follow the same guidelines, don't they?"

Keefe pinned the golden-yellow gargoyle with a questioning look. "What do you mean?"

Lifting his white-clawed hand, Perconz began to count off points on his fingers. "Well, they control certain movements in the city. They often own a large number of businesses. If someone is causing problems with their shit, they remove the obstacle." He shrugged. "Just because we do it for the secrecy of paranormals as opposed to money doesn't make it dissimilar."

"Okay." Keefe could understand that. "But a vampire coven, just like gargoyle clutches, should still be doing it by following the laws of the human world we live in."

The door opened with a ding as Phineas snickered. "Yeah, what makes you think gargoyle clutches or, hell, any paranormal group, don't skirt the law on a regular basis?"

Still grinning, his buddy led the way across the large foyer toward a stairwell. With the garden elevator only taking them to the thirteenth floor, they now had to ascend one floor to reach their rooms on the fourteenth. Opening the door to the stairwell, he led the way inside and began climbing.

"Because it's the right thing to do," Keefe stated firmly. "We live in this world . . . we need to abide by the rules to the best of our ability."

Phineas reached the platform for the next floor and swiped his card, allowing them inside. Holding the door open, he stared at Keefe with concern in his eyes. "And how is us searching for these priests targeting us with the intent of taking them out playing by human laws?" He frowned. "Are you saying we should capture them all and remand them to authorities? Charge them for assault or some bullshit like that so they can go to a human prison?"

Scoffing, Keefe shook his head as he moved past Phineas. "Once a human learns of paranormals, human laws don't apply like you're thinking. If they attack us without provocation, it's self-defense." He frowned, confused at his friend's question. "Besides, it's not like we can tell the authorities, yes, sir, they attacked our business because they think we're a nest of vampires."

"True." Phineas drew the word out. "We can't."

Perconz sighed. "I've lost track of what we're trying to discuss."

Keefe opened his mouth, then snapped it shut again. So had he.

Wait —

"Good," Phineas grumbled, stopping Keefe from saying more. "I'm going to get cleaned up before heading to the coven cafeteria. See you in a bit."

Then Phineas disappeared into his room.

Perconz waved a hand before doing the same.

Keefe followed suit. Originally, he and Phineas had shared a two-bedroom suite, but when Dennis had arrived—a gargoyle enforcer mated to a female vampire—other accommodations were found. Now, they each had their own room, and Dennis had the two-bedroom suite due to his wife expecting the birth of their first-born within the next month.

Shaking his head, Keefe crossed his front room and headed to the bathroom. The lavishly appointed area could be entered either through the front room or the large walk-in closet of the bedroom. Keefe headed in there first to strip off his loincloth, tossing the fabric into his laundry basket. Then he returned to the bathroom and started his evening clean-up routine.

An hour later, after having enjoyed a meal with Phineas and Perconz, Keefe entered the conference room. He greeted Elder Vermidian, who was already there, relaxing on a love seat. His vampire mate, Second Ridger, sat beside him, so Keefe dipped his head by way of hello to him, too.

Taking up his post, Keefe stood behind the elder's sofa. He'd just leaned his shoulder against the wall when Master Krispin entered with several others, including a man he didn't recognize. His attention was immediately drawn to the stranger—a tall, black-haired man with medium-brown skin and a large, thickly-muscled build.

"Are you certain you don't wish to go to the infirmary first, Salem?" Master Krispin was saying. "This meeting can wait."

The stranger—Salem—shook his head. "No, Master Krispin. That isn't necessary." He grinned widely, showing off his fangs. "It's just a scratch." Just as quickly, Salem appeared to sober. "And this information is time-sensitive. We'll need to move quickly in order to capitalize on it."

"Of course," Krispin replied with a nod. "If you're certain."

Salem dipped his chin in another nod, then started toward the sideboard that held an array of drinks.

As Salem moved across the room, the most alluring scent tickled Keefe's nostrils. He inhaled deeply, and his gut clenched. His blood heated and flowed south, and his cock plumped behind his loincloth. Unable to help himself, Keefe inhaled once more before letting out a soft groan.

The noise drew just about everyone's attention, even Salem's, who pinned him with a penetrating, black-eyed stare. The vampire's nostrils flared, and his eyes narrowed. He even let out a low growl, and the corner of his top lip curved up, revealing one fang.

Keefe's heartrate skyrocketed, and not in the way he would have expected upon seeing the feral display. He swept his gaze over Salem's black-clad form. His attention snagged on the left side of the vampire's torso . . . and the heavy blood scent suddenly made sense.

Salem was bleeding.

My mate's been injured!

Roaring with anger, his need to protect and avenge what was his flooding his body with endorphins, Keefe lunged forward. He grabbed Salem's upper arms, holding him in place. The vampire was nearly as broad as himself and almost as tall, and Keefe only had to look down a few inches to peer into his black eyes. Keefe found himself in an answering hold, Salem gripping his upper arms as well.

"Who hurt you, my mate?" Keefe demanded. "I'll kill them."

CHAPTER THREE

Salem stared at the large gargoyle gripping him. While he knew, in theory, that the bigger breed of gargoyles were huge, he'd never interacted with one. To have one looming over him, staring fiercely into his eyes, should have been unnerving.

Except, all Salem felt in that moment was hunger — a deep thirst, his mouth watering with it, for a long, satisfying draw of the gargoyle's blood.

The male's rich, iron flavor called to him in a way none other had before . . . even when Salem had damn near lost his leg from a sword strike.

Then the gargoyle's words registered, and it all made sense.

"I'm your mate." Salem didn't wait for the large, pale-blue gargoyle to confirm his comment. Instead, he added, "That explains why your blood calls to me so badly."

Salem had never taken a lover larger than himself, but the rising craving for the rich fluid pulsing through the male's veins told him that would change very soon.

"Who hurt you?" the gargoyle demanded again.

Right. I was shot.

That also explained his sudden gut-punching thirst. He'd lost a bit of blood and needed to replenish. He'd originally planned to suck down a few bags of blood directly after the meeting.

With his beloved standing right in front of him, Salem realized that wouldn't be necessary.

"Got shot by a priest," Salem stated. With a feral grin, he added, "If you really wanna kill 'em, you'll get your chance." Cutting a quick glance Master Krispin's way, seeing his narrowed eyes and concerned expression, Salem asked, "Permission to have the room for five minutes?"

Master Krispin dipped his chin in confirmation. "Are you certain you don't want more time?"

"This really is time-sensitive, Master Krispin." Salem turned his attention back to the gargoyle who still hadn't released him, but that was fine, since Salem hadn't removed his hands from the other male's upper arms, either. He rubbed his thumbs over the mottled hide, finding the slightly bumpy flesh interesting. "We'll have to bond properly later, gargoyle. We have priests to take out first."

"Understood," the gargoyle rumbled. His pale-gray eyes narrowed as he added, "Protecting my elder and his mate are priority."

Salem grunted, pleased to hear that the gargoyle accepted putting duty first. If he had to be shackled to someone, that they accepted work came first was definitely paramount.

Probably shouldn't think something so uncharitable. A beloved is supposed to be a gift.

Out of the corner of his eyes, Salem saw the room empty. As soon as the door clicked shut behind the last person, he smirked at the larger male.

"We have five minutes, gargoyle," Salem stated. His need to taste the gargoyle was filling him with a single-mindedness. "Take off your loincloth and sit on the sofa."

A low growl rumbled from the larger male. "I'm not having you fuck me on the sofa."

Shaking his head, Salem licked his lips. "No. You're going to feed your mate, help me heal, and you'll love it so much, you're going to spray your seed all over us."

By the time Salem finished talking, he was done waiting. He reached for the stay of the gargoyle's loincloth himself. As he pulled the tie, his soon-to-be lover's lips curved into a hungry smile. After all, Salem was in need — of blood and healing. While he'd intended to wait, meeting his beloved had derailed that plan.

And since he claimed me as his mate, his instinct will be to help, to care for me . . . right?

"If you insist."

Relief flooded Salem upon hearing the gargoyle's words even as his mouth began to water anew.

Then the male finally moved, releasing Salem and taking a step backward. The move tugged the tie from Salem's fingers, and he frowned with displeasure. He followed his beloved's movement, stalking forward.

The gargoyle just smirked as he gripped the tie himself. Within two steps, he pulled the fabric away from his body. Then he tossed it to the other end of the sofa as he relaxed on it.

With his white wings falling over the back of the sofa and his arms spread wide, the gargoyle's thickly muscled body was on clear display.

Salem roved his gaze over what ended up being a gorgeous specimen of maleness. His new lover had miles of muscles beneath his pale-blue, hairless hide. With his legs splayed a bit, his equally blue erection jutted from his groin — long, hard, and ready.

Damn. He has to be at least ten inches.

Recalling that gargoyles bonded by fucking and being fucked, Salem clenched his ass. The male would expect to screw him, too. Salem had never bottomed before. Due to his large size from a very young age, no one had dared ask.

Shit. Can I do that for my beloved?

"This how you want me?"

The gargoyle's words pulled Salem out of his mental freak-out. Snapping his attention to the male's face, he grinned.

"Yes."

Salem moved forward. Resting a knee on each side of the gargoyle, he brazenly straddled him. "Gonna tell me your name before I start our bond?" he asked mildly as he placed his palms back on the gargoyle's upper arms.

Resting his ass on the male's thighs and leaning forward, Salem didn't wait for a response before mouthing over the man's neck tendon.

Grunting, the gargoyle tipped his head to the side, offering Salem more room. "Keefe," he rumbled gruffly. "M'name's Keefe."

Salem hummed in acknowledgment. Then he opened his mouth and sank his fangs deep into Keefe's flesh. Hot succulent liquid, iron-rich and delicious, poured over Salem's tongue. He groaned as his taste buds sang upon experiencing the most amazing flavor he'd ever tasted, quickly going to his head.

Sucking hard, Salem sought for more.

He heard Keefe moan and felt him jolt beneath him. Tightening his hold on Keefe's upper arms, he held him in place as he continued to feed. Heat flooded his body as the influx of blood surged through his veins.

"Fuck!" Keefe rumbled, gruff and low. "Salem."

Keefe jolted once more, and in the next instant, a new scent perfumed the area.

Cum.

Salem smiled around Keefe's flesh, pleased. To his shock, he felt his own cock throb, and his balls began to pull tight. Salem couldn't remember the last time he'd orgasmed from just a feeding, but he was about to now.

Unbuttoning and unzipping his fly, Salem barely had his dick free before he lost control. His release swelled through him, sending his senses soaring. He groaned around the flesh in his mouth as shudders racked his body. His eyes practically rolled to the back of his head as the best damn orgasm of his life crashed through him.

Even as Salem rode those waves, a sharp stab spiked through his shoulder. A second later, the sensation morphed into tingles of delight that washed through his torso to settle in his cock. A second release blindsided him, sending him even higher.

Salem relaxed there, allowing the delicious aftershocks to ping through his system. Finally, he felt Keefe's large hands settle on his hips. The way Keefe massaged lightly into his open pants drew him back to the present.

After sliding his fangs free of Keefe's mottled hide, Salem licked over it. He hummed appreciatively upon seeing the twin fang scars left behind. A wealth of smug satisfaction surged through him.

My mark.

Then Keefe eased his hands higher . . . brushing against Salem's healing wound.

Grunting, Salem straightened, swiftly moving to grip both of Keefe's wrists.

Keefe's pale blue eyebrow ridges furrowed. "Salem?"

Salem grimaced and shook his head. "I'm healing," he assured. "Just still tender is all."

"Are you certain?"

Hearing the concern in Keefe's voice, Salem nodded. "Of course." When his beloved's expression clearly displayed his disbelief, Salem gripped his shirt and whipped it over his head, hissing upon feeling the dried blood tug on his wound. He twisted his torso a little, inspecting the holes. While blood dribbled just a little from the one in his front, Salem could see that the hole was already well on the mend. "See." Grinning, Salem told Keefe, "The blood of a beloved is more potent. I will heal much faster now."

Nice perk, actually.

Keefe growled as he took in the wound. He even looked around Salem's side so he could take in the exit wound. Shaking his head, he frowned at Salem.

"You shouldn't have been injured at all," Keefe grumbled, clearly disgruntled.

Salem scoffed as he began using a clean section of his shirt to clean up the spunk they'd sprayed all over Keefe's torso. The shirt was a total loss, anyway.

"Injuries happen in my line of work, Keefe," Salem stated calmly, meeting the gargoyle's storm-gray eyes. "You're an enforcer. You know that."

Letting out a deep, growling breath, Keefe stared at Salem for a long moment. A tick hitched in his jaw. Then he dipped his chin in a nod.

"I understand," Keefe replied, the admission sounding as if it was torn from him.

Good enough.

Then Keefe moved a hand up and wrapped it around Salem's nape, causing him to freeze. The way the gargoyle applied pressure, urging his head forward, coupled with his focus on Salem's mouth told him of his intentions.

Salem resisted, shaking his head. Upon seeing the obvious question in Keefe's eyes, he explained, "I don't kiss."

Keefe's eyes narrowed. He opened his mouth.

Except, there was a knock at the door followed by Master Krispin calling, "Salem. Keefe. May we come in, or do you need more time?"

Saved by the bell.

"Just a second, Master Krispin," Salem called over his shoulder as he pulled away from Keefe. To his beloved, he stated, "I look forward to being able to continue this later."

"We *will* discuss kissing later, too," Keefe declared even as he released him. He grabbed Salem's shirt as he rose to his feet, finishing his quick wipe down.

Salem didn't comment as he righted and fastened his jeans. There wasn't anything to say, after all.

As Salem moved to open the door, he watched Keefe return

his loincloth to its proper place. Once his beloved was covered—well, as covered as gargoyles seemed to think necessary—Salem opened the door. As everyone filed back into the conference room, the inner circle vampires sniffed and the corners of their lips or eyes crinkled, betraying their amusement, but they didn't say anything. A pale-brown gargoyle smirked and openly winked at Keefe.

Keefe ignored the male while tossing the soiled shirt into a garbage bin.

Then, to Salem's surprise, Keefe crossed to his side and wrapped an arm around his waist while draping a wing over his shoulder.

Salem wasn't certain how he felt about the possessive display, but he didn't comment on it. He even allowed Keefe to guide him to one of the small sofas. When they reached it, Keefe still didn't let go, and he couldn't resist arching one brow in question.

"We have not completed our bond yet," Keefe explained.

Nodding, Salem returned his focus to Master Krispin, who was sitting beside his own beloved on another sofa.

"Are you ready to give your report, Salem?" the master asked.

"Yes, Master," Salem replied. "Upon returning to this area, instead of returning to the coven house, I immediately began following up on the leads of others," he explained. "It's been a couple of months since I've been here, so I'd hoped they wouldn't associate me with the coven."

Second Ridger's lips curved into a wry smile. "That didn't seem to work out quite as well as you'd hoped." He indicated toward Salem's almost-healed torso.

"It did, and it didn't," Salem countered. "I relaxed in the dive bar at the edge of town. The Blue Orchid."

"Stupid name for a dive bar," the same pale-brown gargoyle muttered.

"It was originally a decent honky-tonk bar," Basques stated. "It's changed hands a few times and become quite disreputable, but no one ever changed the name."

Salem resumed his explanation. "I was approached by a couple of guys asking if I was interested in being hired on as muscle for an easy gig." Smirking, he shrugged. "I figured it couldn't hurt to say yes." Salem felt Keefe tense beside him, but he continued. "I followed them to an old farmhouse in the woods. There were plenty of others milling about a dilapidated barn there." With a roll of his eyes, he added, "I'm surprised the last strong wind didn't knock it over."

"Is that the old Miller place?" Master Krispin asked, referring to a man that had died almost two decades before, and no one had been able to track down his grandson.

Nodding, Salem confirmed that. "I was introduced to a couple of other humans, and they started explaining that our job was perimeter watch while the main group finished training to hunt demons." Grinning, he explained, "I laughed and shrugged but agreed. Then I was able to mill around, prop up walls, and listen to many different conversations." Salem growled softly as he explained, "They intend to torch the hotel at midnight. They'll be scattered around the perimeter to mop up the demons as we flee from the building."

"Torch my hotel," Master Krispin snarled. His eyes narrowed, and a low growl filled his words. "With no regard to the innocents within."

"Anyone who consorts with demons aren't innocent." Salem repeated what he'd overheard. With a smirk, he added, "Or so they say."

Keefe frowned at Salem, touching his jaw to get his attention. "And getting shot? How'd that happen?"

"Fiona showed up," Salem revealed, grimacing at being made. It had just been bad luck that he'd walked outside to get some fresh air at that precise moment. "On the back of some black-haired human's motorcycle. Even before parking, she made me. Pulled a gun and started shooting." Growling under his breath, Salem admitted, "Because she was still on the motorcycle, she managed to get close enough to hit me. I made it to the trees, and they couldn't follow."

"Fiona," Keefe snarled, surprising Salem with the intensity of his ire. "That bitch who got away from me."

"You couldn't have known, Keefe." The pale-green gargoyle sitting beside Second Ridger offered Keefe a commiserating smile. "She played us all."

Salem had seen Fiona around the coven house in passing a few times over the years. She was the younger half-sister of their head tracker, Felistria. Fiona was also human, but due to her blood ties to Felistria, they'd allowed her sanctuary. She'd repaid them for their generosity by installing tracking devices on certain vehicles and ratting them out to priests.

So far, no one knew if Fiona had been working with priests prior to joining the coven or if she'd fallen in with them afterward.

Salem looked forward to interrogating her.

CHAPTER FOUR

Keefe barely refrained from issuing another growl. It had been his own folly that had led to his mate being identified and shot. Frustration and guilt rolled through him in equal portions.

Pinning him with a measured look, Salem stared at him. "You feel guilty," Salem mumbled, pitching his voice low. "Why?"

The others had begun to discuss how to defend the hotel from a would-be fire. There was also talk of going to the farmhouse asap to clear out as many as they could before their attempt. Of course, considering Fiona had recognized Salem, there was a slim chance that any priests would still be there. It could be a waste, which just divided their forces.

Answering just as softly, Keefe admitted, "After the fight, we thought Fiona was just a confused human who'd been suckered in by the priests' ideology." He grimaced while shaking his head. "She ran away, and I was ordered to bring her back. I didn't move fast enough. There was a man on a motorcycle waiting for her, and she escaped into the city."

Keefe nodded, humming. "Somewhere you couldn't go because you don't have a human form."

"Correct." Keefe sighed deeply, frowning. "I should have moved faster."

"We all make mistakes," Salem pointed out. "Just like I walked out of the barn at the exact wrong second."

"That was just dumb luck," Keefe countered. "You didn't know."

Salem's chuckle sounded dry. "And how were you to know someone would be waiting on a motorcycle?" He patted Keefe's thigh and added, "All we can do now is figure out how to stop them before they harm others." Even as Keefe processed that, Salem grinned broadly as he loudly cut into others' conversations by saying, "We could trance every human on the street in a five-block radius." He laughed darkly. "See what they know and if they're a priest."

Keefe gaped as he eyed his mate. "You can't be serious."

"Sure. Why not?" Salem cocked his head, his brows furrowing, appearing confused.

"You can't go around trancing every human just to find out if they're involved," Keefe claimed. "Most have no idea about us. That's intrusive."

Salem shrugged. "Whatever works to get information," he countered. "Besides. It's not as if they'll remember."

Keefe gaped at his lover. This was the man Fate decided would be his perfect match? Someone essentially willing to invade the privacy of every human just on the off-chance they were involved.

"Th-That's unethical," Keefe insisted indignantly.

Barking a laugh, Salem grinned at him. "Unethical?" He continued to smile widely, holding Keefe's gaze, as he asked, "How's it any different than a vampire picking up a one-night stand to drink their blood? All they remember is a good time."

Keefe opened his mouth, then snapped it closed again.

How was that different?

Glancing around the room, Keefe realized he had everyone's attention. He noticed the impassive expressions or looks of concern on a number of faces—notably, the vampires—while Vermidian and Phineas eyed him with concern. Keefe had no idea how to respond to that, but the idea of altering people's minds caused his gut to roll uncomfortably.

"Please try to understand, Enforcer Keefe," Master Krispin began slowly. "As a vampire, there are certain things we must accept in order to stay alive. While our laws state never to do a human harm, we do need to feed. Trancing is part of that."

"It's a fact of life," Ridger added from where he held Elder Vermidian's hand.

Rubbing the back of his neck, Keefe tried to reconcile that in his mind, but he couldn't. "I'm sorry," he murmured, shaking his head. "I just . . ." Out of the corner of his eye, he watched Salem, worry filling him. "I just can't seem to get my mind around . . . manipulating someone that way."

Phineas curved his lips into a wry smile. "Well, you're pretty strait-laced, my friend, and you're not a vampire." He lifted one shoulder in a half-shrug. "You weren't raised in this environment. It'll be an adjustment."

An adjustment.

Yeah, right.

Gritting his teeth, Keefe declared, "If someone is a threat to the safety of my elder, the clutch, or my mate, then I will defend to my last breath." He scowled as he shook his head. "Until then, I will not assault an unknown."

Even as Salem's eyes narrowed and his brows drew together, Master Krispin stated, "I can understand and respect your position, Enforcer Keefe." His smile was small, but it was there. "It's always good to stand by your principles." Then Krispin swept his gaze around the room. "I want every enforcer and guard on alert this evening. No one goes anywhere alone. I want teams of three on the streets, keeping an eye on things." His attention turned to Basques. "Use trancing only if they see someone doing something suspicious."

Basques dipped his chin in a curt nod even as his arm tightened on Dloben, his small gargoyle mate. "May I ask for clarification on what is considered suspicious?"

Master Krispin's smile widened aggressively, showing off his fangs. "Anyone with supplies to make large fires. People hiding in the shadows." Smirking, he added, "Someone dodging police or our teams."

Offering a low chuckle, Basques nodded. "I'll pass the word, Master Krispin."

Feeling somewhat mollified, Keefe kept his mouth shut. It wasn't as if he could be one of those out on the street, anyway. First, he didn't yet have a human form. Second, his place was at Elder Vermidian's side.

"I apologize for asking you to delay your bonding, Salem," Master Krispin continued. "But I need you on the streets. You've seen these people. You may be able to recognize them."

"Of course, Master," Salem immediately replied. He turned and met Keefe's gaze. "My apologies, beloved." His dark eyes glittered with something unidentifiable as he reached out and touched Keefe's jaw. "We will make time for us when the danger has passed."

Keefe nodded. "I understand."

He did, too. Duty first. The coven needed to secure their home, and Salem had a job to do.

Master Krispin rose to his feet. "Ridger, with me, please. We're going to check in with Ninevah. I want to make certain everything is up and running." His eyes narrowed. "No room for glitches this evening."

Second Ridger rose from where he'd been seated beside Vermidian. "I'm sure Ninevah will appreciate us checking on him," he stated with a laugh. Then he bent and captured Vermidian's lips, kissing him fast and hard before straightening. "I'll see you soon, my beloved."

"I look forward to it," Vermidian replied huskily. "Call me if you need me."

Ridger nodded. "I will."

After Krispin exchanged a kiss with Wash and Basques did the same with Dloben, everyone began filing from the conference room.

For just an instant, Keefe felt the urge to grab Salem's wrist.

He wanted to pull him back and get his own kiss goodbye. Except, Salem had claimed he didn't kiss, and Keefe had no desire to be rebuffed with an audience.

So Keefe remained silent and still, watching his mate leave without a backward glance.

"Are you okay, Keefe?"

Now alone with the other gargoyles, Keefe turned his attention to Vermidian, and he took a minute to think about the question. "I'm . . . not sure," he admitted softly. "Salem is . . . not what I would have expected in my mate."

Phineas hummed, cocking his head. "I hear Fate gives us what we need, not what we hope for."

Keefe narrowed his eyes as he pinned a hard gaze on Phineas. "And I need a vampire fixer who happily does whatever is necessary to achieve an end?" He couldn't help but growl the words.

Vermidian narrowed his eyes, his features hardening. "Watch it, Keefe," he ordered. "That fixer takes orders from my own mate, so you're dangerously close to insulting Ridger, Krispin, Basques, and their methods."

Letting out a deep breath, Keefe bowed his head. "My apologies, Elder Vermidian. I wasn't thinking."

In truth, Keefe didn't know what to think.

"Perhaps," the elder began slowly. "It would be best to avoid discussions of each of your methods on handling . . . problem situations." He leaned forward, resting his forearms on his thighs. "At least until your bond is complete, until you feel more secure with each other, and you've learned to communicate better."

While Keefe wasn't certain that would help, he still dipped his head in acknowledgment. "Perhaps that would be best, Elder."

"Get to know him as a man," Phineas encouraged. "He appeared to appreciate that you were understanding of his need to be part of taking care of this problem. That's something." Then his brows furrowed, and his next comment sounded almost absent. "I know I'm not the only one who scented the sex you guys had, but he didn't even kiss you goodbye."

Grimacing, Keefe admitted, "He says he doesn't kiss."

"Well, that sucks," Perconz muttered bluntly. "Sharing kisses can be some of the most intimate of experiences with a lover."

Keefe silently agreed.

Keefe hated waiting, but there wasn't much else he could do. After prepping a go-bag—something he knew each of them were doing—they all moved to the roof to wait. As gargoyles, their quickest escape avenue was the skies.

When Wash—carrying the egg incubator—as well as Dloben showed up, Keefe couldn't keep his surprise in check. He would have expected them to be part of the vampire evacuation plan.

Wash must have noticed Keefe's surprise, for he offered him a pinched smile while saying, "Krispin wants me to get our eggling to safety above all else." Sighing roughly, the slender, medium-brown gargoyle rubbed the back of his neck. "I asked him to join me. I can carry them both, but—" Wash shook his head, and Keefe could guess at Krispin's response.

"His place is here, keeping his coven-members safe," Keefe mused softly. "Right?"

With a grimace, Wash nodded.

"Basques told me the same thing," Dloben whispered, wrapping his arms around himself. "But he wants me safe." He nibbled his pale-blue bottom lip as he whispered, "He promised to meet me at the rendezvous point, and he always keeps his promises."

Clustered with the others where they were gathered

around a large metal fire pit, Keefe grumbled, "I can't believe we're considering abandoning the coven's hotel." He glared into the flames, not really seeing them. "This is bullshit. We should have razed the barn, the farmhouse, and any priests in the vicinity."

Phineas scoffed. "How is that different than questioning all the humans on the street?"

To Keefe's surprise, it was Perconz who answered. "We already know that the people at the farmhouse are our enemies," he pointed out. "We know nothing about the average human on the street."

Lifting his hands in surrender, Phineas nodded. "I getcha. I getcha."

"How can we counter what we can't see?" Dloben mused softly, cocking his head.

"What do you mean, Dloben?" Vermidian asked, relaxing in his lawn chair as if he didn't have a care in the world.

Keefe wondered how it would feel to have that much confidence in his mate. As it was, he was almost going out of his mind with worry over Salem. Of course, having a mind link with his bonded vampire probably made all the difference. All the fully bonded gargoyles seemed pretty relaxed, so Keefe decided to take that as a sign that not too much was going on, even though it was nearing midnight.

"Well," Dloben began slowly. "We're gargoyles. We don't deal with priests. We deal with hunters." Resting his hands on his hips, he furrowed his brow ridges over his pale green eyes. "We normally live in sprawling, rural locations, so we can see someone coming from a long way off." Dloben waved his hand in a vacant way, obviously indicating the high-rise rooftop where they waited. "This? This isn't how a gargoyle and a hunter battle. We're out of our depth, and we need to figure out how to adapt."

Growling under his breath, Keefe asked, "Are you saying

we need to figure out how to use computers?" Keefe hated the damn confusing machines. Even his phone was about as old-school as he could get away with.

Shrugging, Dloben pointed out, "It's either figure out how to watch through cameras, get taken by the element of surprise, or we're always going to be dependent on our vampire mates." He crossed his arms over his chest before stating, "I know I'm not a big, winged gargoyle like you guys, but I feel the urge to protect my mate just the same as you."

Vermidian reached over and rested a hand on Dloben's shoulder. "You bring up very valid points." Resting his forearms on his knees, he cocked his head. "Just like you said. How do we fight what we can't see?"

"Maybe we can see them," Keefe countered, staring around the rooftop garden. "We're sitting on the hotel roof of one of the tallest buildings in this small city." He pointed toward the ledge. "We're all paranormals. We have extremely adept hand-eye acuity." While Keefe had never before considered it, he tossed out, "What's to stop us from arming ourselves up here?"

Arching a brow, Phineas tipped up the corner of one lip. "Are you saying we should train to be snipers?"

Dloben gulped so loud it drew attention to his bobbing Adam's apple. "I don't know if I could shoot someone. Hand-to-hand self-defense is one thing, but gunning someone down?" He began shaking his head.

"What about arming yourself with a water hose?" Perconz offered, pointing at a hose the gardener used to water the plants. "If someone tried to set the building on fire, you could point the hose down the building's wall and douse it."

With his green eyes widening, Dloben began to nod, then paused. "But that would leave me in the open. Basques would never go for it."

"He would if we were covering you," Keefe assured, grinning. "We take out anyone aiming at you. We'll keep you safe."

Grimacing, Dennis cut in, "Too bad we didn't think about this before." He peered at his phone before saying, "It's ten after midnight. Think they changed the time or date because Fiona spotted Salem?"

"There's no way to know," Keefe grumbled, still hating the waiting.

"Well, at least we can put our idea into motion," Vermidian claimed with a grin. "I'm going to contact Ridger about getting us some weapons."

"Anything's better than sitting here on our asses," Keefe concluded.

And maybe, I'll have a way to keep an eye on my mate and to keep him safe.

Just that thought caused a bit of his tension to ease.

A few minutes later, Vermidian announced, "Ridger is sending Vicon and Donny up for weapons training."

Keefe smiled, recalling the vampire guards who'd helped them out of a priest ambush right after Vermidian and Ridger had met. The pair had been skilled warriors, and he looked forward to learning from them.

Chapter Five

Narrowing his eyes, Salem leaned against the corner brick façade and stared at the pair of guys a block over. It would have been so easy to slip through the shadows, approach them, then trance them. He could have figured out right away if they were involved.

Except, I can't without probable cause.

Damn beloved already tying my hands and we haven't even bonded yet.

Salem bit back a growl as he shoved away the uncharitable thought.

My beloved is a gift.

Hopefully, Salem wouldn't have to remind himself of that too often. Besides, now that he'd scented and tasted the male, he could feed from no other. Salem had to figure out a way to make it work with him, or he would end up starving to death.

Just then, a third man in a hooded sweatshirt approached from the west. He stopped and talked to the loitering pair. When the man turned to look Salem's way, he was able to see far enough under the hood to make out his face.

Gotcha.

That man Salem recognized.

Lifting his phone, Salem quickly typed out a message to Pierce and Merlick. The first was an enforcer and the latter a tracker. They were patrolling nearby, and between the three of them, they could close in on the trio.

Salem hit send before easing away from the wall. Striding forward, he kept close to the shadows. With his head turned a little, he feigned window shopping while keeping his features hidden and using his peripherals to watch the men.

He knew the instant they spotted him.

The trio stiffened. They glanced between each other. The new arrival whispered something to the others before they split, each walking swiftly in different directions.

While texting Pierce and Merlick, giving them a description of which priest was headed their ways, Salem kept following the hooded man he'd recognized. When he spotted a motorcycle parked ahead, he knew the man was angling for it. After a glance around showed no one else on the street, Salem sprinted forward.

With his vampire speed, Salem was on the man before he even registered that he'd moved. He grabbed him, and with a spin and shove, he pinned him against the brick façade in an alcove. Salem yanked his hood down and peered into blue eyes filled with fear and anger.

"Hello. Marc, isn't it?" Salem rumbled softly, smirking down at the man. "I remember seeing you at the barn."

"Get off me, man," Marc demanded, shoving at his chest, but Salem didn't budge one iota. Scowling up at him, Marc demanded, "If you were at the barn, why are you here? You know we changed the plan because of that infiltrator. We—" Then Marc's eyes widened comically. "Oh, shit! You're him."

Salem grinned widely, showing off his fangs. "Indeed, I am him." Allowing his eyes to haze, he ignored the way Marc began to struggle, flailing and kicking, trying to break free. Salem ignored all that and pushed into Marc's mind. "Now, let's see what you can tell me, Marc."

Marc whimpered and tried to turn his head away, but it was too little, too late. In the next instant, he relaxed in Salem's hold, and his expression grew slack.

Within moments, Salem had stripped Marc's mind of every useful tidbit of information the human had. There wasn't a whole lot. While the guy had thought himself pretty important in what they called *the movement*, he really hadn't been.

Marc hadn't even known where the new meeting site would be. With Salem having been spotted, everyone had been told to go to ground for a few days. They would be contacted via text on where to be for their next meeting.

Salem found the man's memory of Fiona and Erick—the man driving the motorcycle she'd been on—quite amusing.

It seemed, after losing Salem in the forest, they returned to the barn. They'd screamed at everyone for not recognizing a monster right in their very midst. Then they'd located the pair of guys who'd approached Salem in the bar and executed them—as a warning to others, Erick had stated.

Two down, dozens to go.

After that, they'd told everyone that the midnight op was off. Marc and a half dozen others were then tasked with surveillance. They would be replaced at eight AM by others.

Hmmm . . .

While it was tempting to take out Marc on the spot, Salem thought another way might be better. From Marc's memories, he'd gleaned that the man had joined the priests when one of his friend's wives had fallen in love with a vampire, leaving her husband of three years with a sad apology and words about love at first sight as well as a broken heart. Salem guessed that they were beloveds, but without actually meeting the vampire, he would never know.

Marc and his friend—Robert—had followed his then exwife to a restaurant. They'd been on a date. Afterward, they'd spotted the vampire and woman making out in their vehicle after supper, culminating in him feeding from her—hence, they'd learned about vampires.

Salem shook his head at the vampire's stupidity. He was half-tempted to put in the effort of locating the pair and reporting the dude's activity to his coven master. The guy should be reprimanded for his risky behavior at the very least, especially if it turned out that the woman wasn't his beloved.

See, finding your beloved makes you do dumb shit.

But gods, does Keefe taste delicious.

The flavor of the man's blood was almost enough to make him reconsider kissing. *Would the gargoyle's mouth taste just as fine?*

Huh.

See . . . dumb shit.

First, Salem decided he would implant a little impulse of his own. By the time he was done twisting the human's memories, the guy secretly thought what had happened between his buddy's wife and the vampire was the most romantic thing he'd ever heard of. He would never tell his buddy that, though. In fact, Marc was now certain he wanted a vampire to sweep him off his feet like that, and he'd joined the priests in an effort to meet as many of them as he could.

When Salem finally eased out of his mind, he backed up a step and waited. He watched Marc blink a few times, coming out of the lingering effects of Salem's trance.

Marc peered up at him . . . and grinned. "Hey, thanks for meeting me here." He glanced up and down the street, then leaned close and whispered, "Your coven is in the clear tonight. I'll let you know when the new attack is scheduled for."

"Thank you, Marc," Salem replied with a smile. "Your help in securing our safety will not be forgotten."

Nodding eagerly, Marc stepped closer to him. "Then you'll introduce me to some lady vampires, right?"

"Absolutely," Salem agreed. "I never go back on my word. Once your friends are no longer a danger to our people, I'll take you to the cafeteria and introduce you to many single ladies."

Salem could actually think of three particular vampire women that would find Marc attractive. Whether or not they would want anything to do with him once they realized his history . . . well, that remained to be seen.

"Thanks." Marc held out his hand. "I really appreciate it."

Salem took Marc's hand and shook. "Quid pro quo, human."

Marc laughed and nodded. Then he headed toward his motorcycle. As he watched the man swing his leg over before firing it up, he made a mental note to start carrying the burner phone that he'd implanted the phone number of in Marc's mind.

Then Salem watched his new informant drive away.

Smiling, Salem returned to his patrol. He absently wondered what Pierce and Merlick had done with their priests. Firing off a quick text to ask, he strolled down the street, looking for his next victim.

"I'm sorry, you did what?" Master Krispin stared at him, shock filling his pale-blue eyes.

"I turned him into an informant." Salem figured his master's question was rhetorical, but he repeated the information anyway. "If he lives through this situation, he'll be interested in meeting female vampires."

Master Krispin took a swig of his liquor, clearly using the move to try to gather himself.

Ridger, on the other hand, began laughing. The second leaned his forearm on the sideboard, holding his stomach with the other.

Even Basques chuckled low in his throat while shaking his head. That didn't stop the enforcer from saying, "You probably shouldn't tell your beloved about this."

Salem almost opened his mouth to ask why. Just as fast, the answer came to him. His gargoyle's friend had called him strait-laced, and from the sounds of things, he already had a problem with a vampire trancing during feeding.

With a sigh, Salem admitted, "I don't know what Fate was

thinking pairing me with a male such as him."

Krispin managed to pull himself together, for he offered Salem a smile. "Yes, what could Fate have been thinking to pair you with a big, strong gargoyle who can stand by your side and completely understands your commitment to duty?"

Salem rolled his eyes before flopping onto a chair. "You know what I'm talking about," he grumbled as he accepted the tumbler of whiskey from Ridger. "He's the cookie-cutter straight-arrow sort, and I'm the shades of gray." After taking a sip of whiskey, enjoying the mild burn as it settled in his stomach, Salem continued, "Sure, he understands duty, but I'm never going to be able to discuss work with him."

Basques shrugged. "So you'll be like just about every detective, doctor, and psychiatrist out there." Cradling his own drink between both palms, he reminded, "Some fields are just like that."

"Besides," Ridger cut in with a grin. "Maybe Fate thinks you should be a little less gray, or maybe Keefe needs to be a little less straight-arrow." With a wink, he added, "Vermidian asked for some of his people to have training with guns. Maybe Keefe is one of them."

"Guns." Confusion filled Salem. "Why?"

Krispin grimaced. "A city high-rise is not a natural habitat for a paranormal who sleeps as a stone statue during the day and doesn't have a human form until after they've bonded."

Nodding, Basques commented, "They're probably trying to adapt. That doesn't sound like guys who aren't willing to change."

Salem grunted, then downed his drink in one gulp. "Well, I guess I better figure out where my beloved ended up." He rose to his feet and crossed to the sideboard, setting his tumbler on it.

"Yes, you make it sound like such a hardship to spend time with your beloved," Krispin murmured.

Something in his master's tone made Salem snap his attention to the man. He saw the hint of disappointment in his narrowed eyes, and unease slithered through his gut. Salem hated disappointing his master.

Plus, it only took a few seconds to figure out from where it stemmed.

Finding his beloved was supposed to be a time for celebration, but Salem was treating it as if it was a chore . . . something to be tolerated.

"Shit," Salem muttered, scrubbing his hand through his hair. "I'm being an asshole, aren't I?"

"You *are* an asshole, Salem," Ridger stated without a shred of humor. "It's part of what makes you so good at your job."

"In this case," Basques cut in. "You're being a bigger asshole than usual."

Shaking his head, Krispin stated, "And you should never be an asshole to your beloved. You're supposed to protect them from assholes."

Salem nodded once, understanding. "You're telling me to get my head out of my ass."

All three men smiled at him.

After a second of hesitation, Salem offered, "I'll try."

It was the best he could give them.

"That's all anyone can do," Krispin accepted.

Nodding once more, Salem turned toward the door. His hand rested on it when he heard his master speak once more.

"And Salem."

Salem peered over his shoulder at the vampire master.

"Congratulations. It'll be worth it."

"Thank you, Master," Salem replied, then let himself out of the office. He glanced left and right, wondering where he should start looking for his beloved. Sighing, Salem realized he'd just left the people who were most likely to know. He knocked on the door, and when bidden, he popped his head back in and asked, "Uh, any idea where Keefe would be?"

Salem didn't even know where his room was.

"I'll ask Vermidian," Ridger told him before he tipped his head to the side. A smile curved his lips as his eyes turned just a bit vacant, telling him that he was speaking with his lover via their telepathic link. Then he blinked and refocused on Salem. "Vermidian, Keefe, and a few others are in the shooting range."

"Thank you." Salem let himself back out again.

Turning to the left, Salem made his way to the elevator. Once he'd called the car and entered it, he hit the B button—the basement. He had to scan his keycard next, followed by punching in a security code.

The basement contained their security offices, munitions cages, gun ranges, and holding cells.

As Salem rode down to the secure area, he realized he felt something flutter in his gut. It took him a second to recognize the sensation.

Anticipation.

Huh, I'm actually looking forward to seeing my beloved.

Chuckling under his breath, Salem didn't fight the small smile he knew was curving his lips.

CHAPTER SIX

Keefe had never fired a gun in his extremely long life. He'd never thought he would, either. Except, there he was, learning the difference between handguns, rifles, shotguns, caliber rounds, and more. His head swam with information, and he didn't know how he was going to retain it all.

With his large frame, Keefe found certain smaller guns difficult to wield. He thought the scopes on the rifles were fascinating. It reminded him of his telescope, which had been left at Vermidian's estate in Ohio.

Maybe I should have Norad ship it out to me, since I'm going to be here for a while.

As the head of Vermidian's household, Norad had access to every place in the home. He respected peoples' privacy, however, and only entered personal spaces when asked.

I wonder if Salem enjoys stargazing. I think I'll give Norad a call.

Keefe hoped he and his mate could find things in common that they enjoyed.

"Remember to keep the rifle tight to your shoulder," Donny was saying, refocusing Keefe's attention. "The kick can leave a bruise if you don't support it properly." With a chuckle, Donny added, "I've even heard that some of these rifles can break a human's collarbone if used incorrectly."

Arching one brow ridge, Keefe asked, "And yet, they are still used regularly?"

Donny nodded. "Yep. Okay." He gripped the plastic of the ear protection resting around his neck. "Everyone, earmuffs on."

Keefe chuckled as he did as ordered. He had to admit that he appreciated the noise-canceling ear protection. He couldn't imagine the damage the report of these weapons could cause, especially since they were in a gun range hidden below the hotel's underground parking garage.

Using hand signals, Donny indicated for those with weapons to aim and fire.

Even through the protection, Keefe could still hear the faint pop of the rifles. Vermidian and Phineas hit near the bullseye, while Wash's shot went a little wide to the right. Keefe noticed as they continued to shoot, Wash overcompensated to the left before correcting it and hitting center mass.

After the trio had fired a couple of dozen rounds, they lowered their weapons, and everyone took off their ear protection.

"Naturals," Vicon stated with a chuckle. Winking, he added, "It helps to have paranormal reflexes."

"That it does," Phineas agreed. He took a step back and grinned at Keefe. "You're up, Keefe. Let's see what ya got."

Keefe allowed his lips to twitch, betraying his amusement at Phineas's playfulness. "Bet I hit the center of the bullseye on the first shot," he told his friend.

Phineas's deep brown eyes narrowed. "Oh?" A sly expression creased his features. "And if you fail, you have to watch *Survivor* with me."

Growling under his breath, Keefe stated, "No fucking way."

Crossing his brown arms over his chest, Phineas snickered. "What? You scared?"

Keefe sneered at the other gargoyle, his natural competitiveness surging. "Fine." He strode forward, taking Phineas's place at the firing range. "If I win" — then he amended — "*when* I win, you'll watch a space documentary with me."

Phineas smirked. "You're on." Then he grinned broadly.

"But you won't win."

Taking his place where Phineas had been, Keefe watched a chuckling Donny change out the paper targets. Perconz took over Vermidian's station while Dennis took over Wash's. Once ready, with their ear protection back in place, Keefe lifted his rifle.

Finding the target through his scope, Keefe took slow deep breaths. He focused on the crosshairs that represented a head-shot. After getting the okay from Donny's countdown, Keefe took one more breath, let it out slowly, and fired.

Keefe continued looking through the scope ... and grinned.

Spot on.

Continuing to fire, Keefe pegged the target over and over. He knew he'd won the bet, and the rest of his shots were simply for practice. To his pleasure, Keefe realized he would have made a damn good sniper had he been so inclined.

Once Keefe emptied the clip, switched it out for a second one, and fired those, too, he lowered the weapon and placed it on the platform. Looking left and right, he saw that the others had done well, too ... although not as well as himself. Soon, Vicon signaled it was safe to remove his ear protection, so he did.

Keefe turned and grinned at Phineas. "I win. Space documentary at my place at my choosing."

Phineas groaned good-naturedly. "Fine, fine."

"You like space documentaries?"

Looking left, toward the entrance, Keefe spotted Salem standing there. His breath caught for a second as he took in his mate. Somehow, Keefe found Salem even more breathtaking than before.

Salem filled out his black jeans to perfection. His thigh-length leather jacket stretched across his broad shoulders. Even his short black hair called for Keefe to scrap his nails over Salem's scalp.

Stunning.

"Yeah, Keefe has a telescope back home," Phineas answered for him. "He loves that type of shit."

Keefe felt heat rise along his neck, and he prayed it didn't show as a blush.

To Keefe's surprise—and pleasure—a small smile curved Salem's full, dark lips, and he claimed, "I enjoy them, too. Perhaps we can compare which ones we've seen."

Huh. Something in common.

"In fact," Salem continued, moving toward him, his focus pinned on Keefe as if he didn't even see the others in the room. "I even have a telescope. I know a killer spot for stargazing a little ways out of town." His smile somehow seemed to warm his deep black eyes. "Perhaps, if we can find a spare moment, it would be fun to take a picnic, set up my scope, and get to know each other."

Keefe nodded. "I would enjoy that very much."

Salem smiled widely, showing off his fangs. "Perfect." Then his attention finally flickered around to everyone. "How's the training going? Anything I can help with?"

"We're just running through the last of the rifles we keep in supply, Enforcer Salem," Donny told him, dipping his head just a smidge in deference to the higher-ranking vampire. "As expected, with their paranormal gifts, they picked it up pretty quickly."

Chuckling, Vicon added, "Although a few of the smaller handguns are a bit small for their large hands to use comfortably." He lifted his own hand and wiggled his fingers as if in emphasis.

Salem glanced at Keefe's hands before meeting his gaze again. "Makes sense." There was the unmistakable gleam of hunger in his eyes. "But I bet they'd feel damn fine sliding over my skin." With another wide smile, Salem asked, "Are you about done here? Think you can get away for a bit?"

Keefe felt his blood heat, and there was no mistaking the

way Salem was eyeing him. His mate wanted something of the carnal variety. Keefe was more than on board with that.

Except—

Clearing his throat, Keefe tore his gaze away from his sexy vampire in order to glance at Vermidian. He met Salem's eyes again and stated, "My shift ends in about an hour. Then I'll have a couple of hours before sunrise forces me to roost." That didn't really leave them much time, but—"I would enjoy spending that time with you."

"Nonsense, Keefe," Vermidian countered, clapping him on the shoulder. "Go with your mate." He waved his hand toward the others. "I'm well protected. You need this time to grow your bond."

Keefe opened his mouth, hesitating. As much as he wanted to spend as much of the remaining evening with his mate as possible, he was there to do a job.

Salem seemed to have no such hang-up. "Thank you, Elder," the vampire rumbled. Reaching out a hand, he gripped Keefe's wrist and tugged to get him moving. "I know we both appreciate your understanding."

"Don't forget to explain cinnamon!" Phineas called with a laugh as Keefe found himself being led back toward the elevator.

Growling, Keefe hollered, "I'll collect on that debt another time, Phineas."

Phineas just laughed as Salem led Keefe into the elevator box.

Once the doors closed, Salem pressed a floor button—eighteen—then used a keycard and entered a code. Keefe knew the keycard and code entered would make it so the car would not stop at any floor where uninitiated humans could be—starting at the underground parking, to the main floor at ground level, which contained the hotel check-in, a nightclub, and a lounge, then all the standard hotel rooms for humans up to the twelfth floor. The car started moving, and he eased close and rested his palms on Keefe's chest. He rubbed up and down, mapping his torso.

The sensual glide caused Keefe's brain to begin to short-circuit. Lust and pleasure infused his body in equal measure. His mouth watered with his desire to taste Salem—not just his mouth, but every bit of flesh, too.

"I'm not usually a touchy-feely or tactile person," Salem rumbled, sounding almost confused. "But your skin, well, I really like the feel of it." Before Keefe could come up with a response—one that would most likely have been, *it's a mate thing*—Salem continued, "And what's this about cinnamon?"

Keefe rested his palms on Salem's hands, ceasing their petting. Squeezing lightly, he managed to get his brain to engage. "Are you aware that a gargoyle can impregnate his male fated mate?"

For an instant, Salem appeared shocked. Then he scoffed and nodded. "Yes, right. Forgot about that." He offered a small smile as he added, "That's how Master Krispin ended up with their egg." Then Salem's features blanched. "You don't expect me to, uh—" He finished by shaking his head. "Just no."

Relief flooded Keefe, and he couldn't help but chuckle softly. "Your reaction has afforded me the greatest of relief, my mate," he admitted. "I have no wish for children, either."

Blowing out a breath of obvious relief, Salem nodded. "Gods, you had me worried for a minute there." He scoffed, his smile turning wry. "I mean, more power to Wash and my master, but damn. Raising kids has never been a blip on my radar, and I tend to avoid them. Or scare them, although not on purpose." Keefe joined Salem in a soft chuckle before his mate asked, "So, uh, how do we stop me from getting knocked up." Clearing his throat, he added, "Um, once I get up the nerve to accept your cock and all."

Keefe knew he would have to address that comment later. "Cinnamon is a natural contraceptive to just about every gargoyle's sperm," he explained. "I take cinnamon in my coffee every morning."

"So, you're sterile."

Nodding, Keefe told him, "As long as I eat cinnamon, I'll remain sterile."

"What happens if I eat cinnamon?"

"The same result," Keefe told him. "Whatever chemical is in cinnamon that renders us sterile will affect you, too. With it in your bloodstream, even if I forgot, my semen would be unable to cause you to conceive."

Salem nodded once. "Okay then. Sounds like I'm gonna eat a cinnamon roll with my coffee each morning."

Surprised at the statement, Keefe couldn't help the way he stiffened or tightened his hold on Salem's hands. "You don't trust me?"

Shaking his head, Salem told him, "That's not it at all, Keefe." The car stopped, and he pulled away as the door opened. "You see" — he continued, leading the way down the hall — "I'm of the belief that it takes two people to make a kid, which means it's the responsibility of both people to *not* make a kid. We both do our part." Salem stopped at the door of a suite. Before opening it, he focused on Keefe and stated, "For example, even if a woman told me she was on the pill or used some other contraceptive, I still used a condom. No condom, no sex." Shrugging, he scoffed. "Well, with anyone, really, but the same principle applies. I do my part."

Hearing Salem talk about fucking women sent a riot of jealousy surging through Keefe. He growled low in his throat as he grabbed his mate's hip with one hand. With his other, Keefe grabbed Salem's neck.

"You're mine," Keefe snarled, right before he slammed his lips over Salem's own.

Keefe didn't ask. He took. He thrust his tongue between his clearly surprised mate's lips. Swirling his appendage around, he sank deep, tasting and mapping. Keefe teased along his tongue, licked over his gums, and swiped along first one fang, then the other.

Salem's taste exploded across Keefe's tongue, rich and masculine with the hint of good whiskey, and he couldn't seem to get enough. He ravished Salem, needing more, needing everything.

It took Keefe a minute to register the claws digging into his upper arms. In response, he gentled the kiss, licking and sipping at Salem's lips. He realized his vampire wasn't truly participating, letting Keefe do all the work.

That was when he recalled Salem's claim. He didn't kiss.

Disappointment stabbed through Keefe's gut, and he began drawing the kiss to an end. As he was about to lift his head, Salem suddenly groaned, startling him. Then his mate tipped his head just a bit and began kissing Keefe back.

Salem slid his right hand up Keefe's arm and threaded his fingers into his hair. Tangling his fingers in his long hair, he scraped his talons ever-so-lightly along his scalp. He used the hold to position Keefe right where he seemed to want him, then did a little exploring of his own.

Keefe happily went along for the ride, accepting Salem's probing tongue and suckling on it lightly.

Finally, when Keefe worried he might pass out from lack of oxygen, Salem jerked back, breaking the kiss.

Panting harshly, Keefe stared down at Salem. He admired the way his mate's chest rose and fell, also gasping for breath. His full dark lips were kiss-swollen, and his eyes were tinged with red, betraying his desire.

"Well, fuck," Salem muttered gruffly. "Guess I'm gonna reconsider that kissin' thing."

Giving his mate a feral grin, Keefe declared, "Good." Then

he recalled what had brought it all on in the first place. Curling his lip, Keefe declared, "No fucking anyone but me, so condoms are no longer necessary. You're mine."

Salem stared at him with a startled expression for a second. Then he grinned broadly. "As if anyone could compare to my beloved." He smirked as he added, "You know I'll never get a boner for another. We're it for each other."

In Keefe's rational mind, he had known that. Once paranormals mated, that was it. They never had sex with another, and there was no chance for divorce. That was the way of the paranormal.

Still, they could obviously get jealous.

Keefe took in a deep breath, then let it out through pursed lips. "Yes. Yes, I do know that." Unable to help it, he smiled crookedly at Salem. "But hearing you talking of fucking others"—he squashed the renewing wave of possessive jealousy—"really pissed me off, so don't do that." Seeing Salem's eyes narrow slightly, Keefe quickly added, "And thank you for the explanation about cinnamon. I understand now."

Salem continued to stare for a few seconds before he nodded. "Okay. Uh, please offer me the same courtesy. No talk of fucking others."

"Done," Keefe pledged.

"Um, hey, uh, Enforcer Salem," a timid voice interrupted, coming from their left.

Turning to look that way, Keefe took in a slender, blond-haired vampire. He was shorter than average—maybe five-foot-six. He had his arms wrapped around himself, and he shifted uneasily from foot to foot. His blue eyes held a wealth of uncertainty and even a little trepidation.

"Yes, Jethro?" Salem answered, obviously knowing him.

"Um, I know I'm not supposed to touch a gargoyle's wings, it bein' rude and all." Jethro cast a glance toward Keefe's wings before meeting Keefe's gaze and saying, "But you have yours spread, and they're blocking the hall, and I can't get past to go to my suite."

"Shit," Keefe mumbled, embarrassment flooding him at his loss of control. He swiftly lowered his wings, folding them and draping them over his shoulders. "My apologies."

Salem chuckled as he pulled away and opened his door. "Sorry about that, Jethro," he called after the vampire who was scurrying past and down the hall. "New beloved and all."

With a squeak in his voice, Jethro hollered, "Congratulations," before disappearing into a room a ways down the hall.

Grinning, Salem led the way into his rooms. "Come on."

Chapter Seven

Salem couldn't remember the last time he'd kissed someone. As a loner who didn't care much for company, he'd always taken his sustenance from one-night stands. Even when young, he'd been larger and far more intimidating than other vampires—both in size and attitude.

At that time, Salem's bed-partners had been those thinking they were taking a walk on the wild side. There had been no kissing. Salem hadn't had a problem with that.

He also hadn't realized what he'd been missing.

Salem was surprised to feel relief that Keefe had pressed the issue. The taste of his gargoyle's mouth had been almost as delicious as his blood. His cock had gone from hard to straining in the blink of an eye, and he'd nearly come in his jeans—something he had never done before.

Leading Keefe to his bedroom, Salem admitted, "I'm not one for romance, so if you want wine and roses, I'll try to figure that shit out later." He released his gargoyle's hand in favor of sliding out of his coat. "Right now, I'm hard as nails, and I want to fuck you," Salem declared, licking his lips as he swept his gaze over Keefe's big body. His attention snagged at the massive erection tenting his gargoyle's loincloth. Returning his focus to Keefe's pale-blue face, he asked, "That okay with you? To get our bond started?"

Keefe smirked at him. Instead of replying verbally, he tugged his loincloth free of his body and tossed it onto a nearby chair.

Salem growled as he eyed his beloved's stunning erection.

"Perfect."

"My answer? Or my cock?"

Barking a laugh, Salem yanked his shirt over his head. He continued to smile as he stripped in record time. "Both," he declared with a wink.

"Hmmm." Keefe pinned a feral gaze upon him. "Good. Where's your lube?"

"Nightstand," Salem teased. "Where else?"

"Excellent location," Keefe replied, crossing to the afore-mentioned piece of furniture. "Got any toys in here you like to play with?" he asked, retrieving the lube before he brazenly rummaged through the drawer.

Salem chuckled as he shook his head. "Not a toy guy."

"Pity." Keefe stopped looking and turned to crawl onto the comforter. He made himself comfortable, relaxing on his back with his wings stretched out beneath him and his legs slightly spread. "But on the other hand, I'll enjoy introducing you to certain things."

Waggling his brows, Salem climbed up onto the bed near Keefe's feet. "Really?" He pushed Keefe's legs wider, and his beloved moved willingly. "What sort of things?"

"Hmmm . . ." Keefe placed the lube on the mattress beside his hip, then rested his hands behind his head, spreading himself out for Salem's viewing pleasure. "Well, I guess it will all depend on your sensitive points."

"Oh?" Salem grabbed the lube and popped it open. "Like what?"

As Salem poured a liberal amount of lube onto the fingers of his left hand, he took in Keefe's musing expression. It suddenly hit him that he couldn't remember the last time he'd shared a conversation with a lover, let alone exchanged teasing comments. He was already enjoying what they were doing more than the best fuck he could recall.

Damn. I've had a sterile love life.

As Salem teased his fingertips over Keefe's hole, he realized that would no longer be the case.

Fate must be blessing me after all.

"Well," Keefe murmured as his chute sucked in Salem's first finger. "If your nipples are sensitive, I suggest clamps." He rocked his hips provocatively as Salem eased his finger out, then in again. "Or piercings." Licking his lips, Keefe pinned a heated gaze on Salem's chest, and his eyes narrowed. "I can just imagine the fun of sucking silver barbells as you writhe beneath me."

Salem sucked in a sharp breath, and his dick twitched. He'd never considered his nipples extremely sensitive, but he did enjoy playing with them when he jacked off. He could only guess at how it would feel for them to be licked or nipped.

Another something that would be new.

"Oh, it sounds as if you like that idea," Keefe murmured, his voice growing gruff. "Or if your balls are sensitive, how would it feel to have them shaved?"

Barking a laugh, Salem shook his head at that one. "Hard no, gargoyle." Even as he took in his beloved's arched brow and challenging expression, he shook his head again. "Not happening."

Then, to distract Keefe, Salem pushed a second finger into his beloved's chute. The hot muscle squeezed his fingers so good, and his cock jerked once more as Salem's anticipation ramped up. Crooking his fingers, he searched . . .

Keefe groaned, and his hips jolted. "Fuck, Salem," he muttered. "Fuck, right there."

"Yeah, we're gonna be fucking, all right," Salem responded on a growl. "Gonna sink my dick in your tight ass and fuck you into orgasm."

As Salem spoke, he pushed another finger into Keefe's channel, fucking him with three. To ease the sting, he continued to rub over his prostate, stimulating his gland as he stretched his beloved.

"Now, Salem," Keefe demanded, lifting his hands to reach for him. "I'm ready."

Salem hesitated for an instant, then decided to take Keefe at his words. Pulling his fingers free, he quickly drizzled more lube onto them. Then he greased up his erection before guiding it to the gargoyle's prepped hole.

Levering over the larger male, resting his weight on his hand, Salem ordered, "Push out, Keefe. I want in you." Then he thrust.

With hardly any pressure, Keefe's body gave way. Salem slid in and in and in, sinking deep into the hottest, tightest channel he'd ever before experienced. He kept his gaze riveted on where he penetrated his gargoyle, the blue skin having lightened nearly to white with the way his dick stretched it was the most erotic sight he could ever recall.

Once Salem's balls rested against Keefe's ass, he forced his body to freeze. His breaths came in ragged pants, and shock slithered through him when a bead of sweat dripped down his temple, his body so hot just from the penetration. Lifting his gaze from where he joined with Keefe, Salem stared deep into his beloved's storm-gray eyes for several long seconds.

Keefe slowly smiled, a flush pinking his blue cheeks. "Move," he urged, lifting his arms to grip Salem's upper arms in a familiar hold. "Make me yours."

Salem curled his lips in a feral smile. "You're already mine, Keefe," he declared. "This is just a formality."

Then Salem began to move. He withdrew until his cock nearly popped free before reversing direction. The heat and pressure went straight to his balls, and he couldn't help but speed up—faster and faster.

The sound of Keefe's moans joined with Salem's grunts. Their bodies fired hotter and hotter, and sweat oozed between them. Keefe's erection, pinned between them, slid deliciously across Salem's abdominals. Even the slap, slap of their bodies against each other mingled to create the most erotic cacophony.

It so quickly went to Salem's head that his balls began to pull tight. Wanting, needing Keefe to fly over that edge first, he reached between them and gripped his dick. Squeezing hard and jacking in time with his thrusts, Salem ordered, "Come for me, my gargoyle."

As if hardwired to obey, Keefe did just that. He arched his neck as he roared, exposing the long line of his throat. The blissful cry echoed off the walls as Keefe's cock jerked and swelled in his grip.

The fragrant scent of cum perfumed the air, making Salem's mouth water for more than just blood.

Then Salem's nature took over. He slammed his erection as deeply as he could go and stilled as his orgasm swelled over him. Opening his mouth, he sank his fangs into his claiming scar. He heard Keefe's grunt as he licked around his embedded teeth, wiping away the sweet nectar that was his gargoyle's blood.

The big body beneath him shuddered once, twice, and more seed dampened the space between them while Salem continued to pump his lover full of his jizz, marking him inside and out.

Gently, Salem eased his teeth from Keefe's flesh. After licking, clearing away the last few drops of blood, he rested his weight on his left arm. Salem peered into Keefe's eyes, pleased to see the heavy-lidded satiation in them.

For the first time ever, Salem didn't feel the desire to pull away from his lover. He wanted to lie still and stroke his hands over every inch of skin he could reach. Salem couldn't remember the last time he'd explored a lover, but this was his beloved.

Perhaps that made all the difference.

As Salem gave in to his urge, stroking his palm down Keefe's side and along his ribcage, he struggled with what to say. He'd never been a chatty person, and he found himself at a complete loss as to what to say. Salem rested his elbow on the comforter and relaxed against Keefe as he touched him with his other hand.

To Salem's pleasure, Keefe didn't seem to need him to say anything. The gargoyle slid his palms from Salem's arms, up around his back. He petted over his flesh, exploring the knobs of his spine.

For several long minutes, they lay together—touching, exploring, and just breathing in each other's essence.

Keefe eventually reached Salem's crease and dipped one finger in, teasing his sensitive flesh.

Salem couldn't help it. He clenched.

Obviously feeling it, Keefe arched one eyebrow ridge in silent question.

Blowing out a breath, Salem admitted, "I've never been fucked."

Keefe smiled, the expression turning hungry. "Then I will be the only one to ever know such joy."

Swallowing hard, Salem admitted, "I'm just not certain when I'll be able to work up to that." He scowled, rubbing the back of his neck. "And I know that's the fastest way for you to molt. Like, as in"—he glanced toward his nightstand, checking the time—"around an hour and a half."

When his coven's inner circle had begun finding their beloveds in gargoyles, a lot of information had been passed around the coven. After a gargoyle bonded—by claiming and being claimed by their mate—they would go through a process called molt. Evidently, it was a painful first shift that gave them a human form. Fortunately, after that, they could shift at will, and it wouldn't harm them.

"Would you be averse to me playing with your prostate?"

Keefe asked, cocking his head a bit as he eyed him. With a smile toying at the corners of his lips, he added, "You could stay right where you are, and I would use my tail. We make out like randy teenagers while I drive you out of your everloving mind."

Scoffing softly, Salem admitted, "I never made out, even when I was a randy teenager."

"Oh?" Keefe picked up the lube and poured a healthy dollop onto the first several inches of his tail. After closing it and placing it on the bed, Keefe used his palm to coat his tail properly. "Tell me." He met Salem's gaze once more. "What was Salem Galdesque like as a teenager?"

Then Keefe brought his tail up and curled it over Salem's butt cheek. Just the tip began to wiggle between his mounds, the appendage slick and agile.

Taking a slow, deep breath, Salem fought against his urge to clench. He took the topic Keefe offered, knowing it was a distraction. Salem thought back to those days, oh-so-long ago.

"Well," Salem began slowly. "I was born over two hundred years ago in what is now the Congo."

"Hmmm," Keefe mused. "You're a long way from home."

Salem lifted one shoulder in a half-shrug. "My father was a vampire. My mother was human." Recalling them, he had to smile. "They were good parents, and when I was younger, I remember them being happy."

Keefe pressed his tail a bit deeper as he asked, "What changed?"

"Me," Salem admitted, the familiar frustration and sadness filling him. "I had a major growth spurt when I was fifteen, and suddenly, the coven master started seeing me as a threat."

Frowning, Keefe murmured, "I'd hoped to distract you, not upset you."

Shaking his head, Salem told him, "It's fine." He swallowed hard before saying, "I think you teasing my prostate, which is supposed to be damn relaxing, would be an enjoyable distraction as I relay this next bit."

Salem even spread his legs a little wider in invitation.

Keefe arched one brow, but he did as Salem requested, taking him at his word. Salem appreciated that about his gargoyle. He accepted what he said.

Sliding his tail along the sensitive flesh of his inner trench, Keefe teased at skin no one else had ever touched. To Salem's surprise, it felt . . . good. When Keefe's tail massaged his entrance, it sent odd zings through him that even warmed his balls.

Huh.

When Keefe pressed into him, Salem breathed through the breach while murmuring, "The master decided humans could no longer be in his coven, so he kicked out my parents, me, and one other couple." He moved his head to rest against Keefe's chest and slid his palms to his gargoyle's shoulders. He'd never had a lover large enough for him to lie on, and it was a novel experience for him. Of course, he'd never had a lover he wanted to lie with at all, but that was beside the point to him.

"Did you all find a new coven to join?" Keefe whispered the question just as his tail ghosted over Salem's gland.

The warm shockwaves it created flooded his groin, and his cock actually twitched where it was still embedded within Keefe's body.

Humming, Salem mumbled, "No. My mother was captured by slavers and shipped to America."

Keefe froze. "Fuck."

"Don't stop," Salem urged, tipping his head up a little to eye Keefe.

His beloved's jaw was tight, but he continued his ministrations. He worked on Salem's prostate, gently stimulating him, pleasuring him.

"My father found us passage here." Salem frowned. While his memories of the voyage were hazy, he recalled it had been terrible. Too many humans clustered together, many of them growing sick. "Dad found Mom, freed her, but then we had to hide out west. There were no covens out here at that time, and it was hard." Holding Keefe's gray-eyed gaze, Salem told him, "Eventually, we found Krispin's coven here, and he took us in. That was about a hundred years ago, and I will forever be grateful that he didn't turn us away just because of my size."

Sighing, Keefe smiled in obvious relief. Then he winked and asked, "So, am I going to have to meet the parents at some point?"

Salem chuckled softly before he groaned, a fresh wave of amazing tingles zinging through his bloodstream. "No," he managed to get out. "Th-They died, ugh"—he clenched and released his hands on Keefe's shoulders, trying to fight his sudden desire to rut—"s-sixty plus years ago." Giving up the fight, Salem began to move within the confines of Keefe's body. "Fucking hell, Keefe." His gargoyle managed to work his gland, fucking him in counterpoint with his tail. "Why haven't I done this before," Salem panted. "T-Totally missed out."

Keefe grinned widely, eyes dark with his own need. "Because you were waiting for me." He pressed harder on Salem's gland, demanding, "Come for me, Salem. Then I'm going to flip you around and plow your gorgeous ass, bonding us for eternity."

Nodding, Salem picked up his pace. He was more than on board with that.

Chapter Eight

"Stop being such a pussy and unlock the damn door!"

Keefe fought to keep in his groan, but he knew he'd failed. His body shuddered of its own accord. His arms gave out, and he landed face-first onto the tile of the bathroom floor.

Surprisingly, the cold tile felt fantastic against his sweaty cheek . . . for a few seconds anyway. Then a fresh ripple of painful tendrils spread over the skin of his body.

Even knowing what was happening, Keefe still felt a fissure of unease slide through him.

Gods, why is this so painful? Is it supposed to be like this?

"Keefe," Salem called again. "I said open the door, damn it."

Finding his tongue, Keefe managed to say, "I-I'll be fine." He swallowed hard, hating how weak he sounded. "Just a minute."

Gods, I hope it won't be more than a minute.

Only Keefe's sensitive hearing allowed him to make out Salem's grumbled, "Like hell I'll give you a minute."

Then Keefe heard the grind of locked tumblers being forced, and he glared toward the door. "J-Just leave me—argh."

As Keefe watched the doorknob turn, spikes of agony shot up his fingers, as if someone was attempting to tear out his claws. Spots appeared before his vision, and he roared with anguish.

"Fucking hell, Keefe." Salem's voice came from right beside him. "Why are you trying to do this on your own?"

Keefe had several answers that he wished he could give.

I didn't want you to see me like this.

Many mates had commented on how scary it seemed.

Some think the first change is gross.

Except, Keefe could only focus on clenching his teeth to cut off his screaming. He dragged in one pain-filled breath at a time, all the while praying for relief from any god who cared to listen.

Then . . . it happened.

Blessed relief—on his hands anyway.

Peeling open his eyelids, Keefe realized Salem was straddling his back, and he'd wrapped his fingers around Keefe's own. Then he carefully sprawled on top of him. The large vampire almost managed to cover him completely, and everywhere he touched, the pain became muted.

Keefe could still feel it, but it wasn't nearly as debilitating. Instead, the sensations were more tingling pinpricks as opposed to shards of agony. He managed to breathe a little easier and sighed with relief.

"H-How?" Keefe whispered roughly. "What?"

Salem nuzzled his cheek against the back of Keefe's neck, which felt oddly amazing. "Didn't you know that your mate's touch eases the agony of molt?"

Huh.

Furrowing his brow ridges, Keefe admitted, "No. I missed that."

"The Aerasceatle clutch passed on the information when Basques bonded with Dloben," Salem told him, releasing his fingers so he could run his hands up and down his arms. "I hear Ridger is damn proud of himself because he actually made Vermidian orgasm during the event."

Gaping, Keefe turned his head enough to meet Salem's gaze. "How the fuck—" He paused to grunt as his shoulder blades felt as if they were being stabbed.

Salem lowered his head to lick and nip over the skin of one

wing while massaging the other with a hand. In seconds, the sensation eased a little, and then Keefe felt the oddness of having no wings at all. He knew they must have been retracting into his back for the first time.

"The gossip vine tells that Ridger fucked Vermidian through it." While mirth filled Salem's tone, he quickly added, "And everyone has been forbidden of speaking about it to Vermidian. Understandably, our second doesn't want his beloved to be embarrassed." Then Salem nipped at Keefe's ear before huskily whispering, "But just think, that could have been us, my cock soothing your ass from the inside when your tail retracted for the first time, us both comfortable in a bed instead of on this cold bathroom floor. Silly, stubborn beloved."

"S-Sorry," Keefe muttered. "If I'd known."

"We're going to have to have your elder send out a clutch-wide memo," Salem commented as he continued to rub all over Keefe's body. He even rubbed his legs back and forth over Keefe's, trying to reach every bit of skin that he could.

Finally, the last of the sensations passed.

Keefe let out a deep, heartfelt sigh, finally able to relax. Of course, as Salem had pointed out, the hard tile of the bathroom floor wasn't the most comfortable place to do that.

"How are you feeling?" Salem asked before licking over the claiming mark he'd left on Keefe's neck. "Better?"

Nodding, Keefe whispered, "Better." After clearing his throat, he added, "Thank you."

"You're my beloved, Keefe." Salem said it calmly, matter-of-fact. "I know I can be a bit of an asshole, but that doesn't mean I want you hurting unnecessarily. I still have the same instincts to care for and please my beloved."

Curving his lips into a small smile, Keefe realized he'd heard those words not too long ago, and they warmed something deep in his heart, making his gut flutter.

Before Keefe could figure out any kind of response, Salem slid off of him and pushed to his feet. "Let's get you in the shower," he stated, suddenly sounding a bit gruff. "You're sweaty, and not for a good reason."

Then the sound of the shower began.

Wet, naked mate?

Keefe didn't need to be asked twice. Unfortunately, when he tried to push to his feet, he didn't have the strength. Swaying, he grabbed onto the edge of the counter to keep from collapsing back to the floor.

"Shit," Salem muttered, wrapping his strong arms around him.

With his face pressed against Salem's torso, Keefe was able to get a deep whiff of his vampire. He caught lingering traces of concern, worry, and even a bit of frustration. He also scented embarrassment, which confused him.

Then Keefe wondered when the last time Salem had shared anything remotely sentimental with someone. He wasn't going to ask, and he bet Salem wouldn't share.

That's okay. Not everything needs to be voiced.

Keefe happily allowed Salem to guide him into the shower. As he stood propped up against the wall, he discovered something else. In Keefe's human form, they stood the same height — six-foot-five — which meant he'd lost five inches. His frame remained thickly muscled, however, so that was good.

"I love that you still have your long, white hair," Salem commented as he washed it. "It's great for holding your head at the perfect angle so I can kiss you the way I want or hold your head off to the side while I fuck you so I can sink my fangs deep into your neck."

Upon hearing those words, Keefe went from relaxed and content to hot, hard, and horny in under two seconds.

"Yes, please." Keefe refused to think of that as begging.

That was okay because Salem still gave him exactly what he wanted, sinking deep into his body and having his way with him.

While what a person looked like—whether or not they were aesthetically pleasing—had never been a worry for Keefe, he did wonder about some of the looks they were getting.

After the shower, Salem had asked if he wanted to check out the restaurant on the second floor, which afforded a lovely view of the nearby river. It would allow him to see the sun glittering off the small waterfall as they enjoyed a meal together. Keefe had found the idea refreshing, and he'd happily agreed.

Now, Keefe thought perhaps they'd made a mistake.

As they walked through the restaurant to the table by the windows that Salem had requested from the vampire hostess, a number of humans—male and female—turned their heads to watch them. When Keefe met their gaze, they would hurriedly look away, sometimes even leaning over to whisper with whoever they were dining with.

Being a paranormal, Keefe picked up on a number of the comments.

Did you see those guys?

God, look at his eyes.

Do you think his hair is natural?

Taking the seat the hostess indicated, Keefe waited until she'd left to lean on the table and mutter, "We're drawing attention. Am I not dressed properly or something?" Keefe was wearing clothes similar to others he'd seen—jeans and a polo shirt.

"Not at all." Salem didn't sound concerned in the least. He picked up his menu and stared down at the offerings as he added, "You're a sexy as fuck man, and they're all staring because they find you attractive."

"They—Really?" Keefe couldn't keep the surprise out of his voice.

Salem lifted his focus from his perusal of the menu. Evidently, whatever expression Keefe sported drew a heated smirk to his face. "Oh, Keefe," he rumbled, reaching across the table to lay his hand over Keefe's own. "Yes, my beloved." Keeping his voice pitched low, Salem continued, "Humans will find you extremely desirable. Your eyes, your hair, your well-muscled build. You're what's called a silver fox, and they find that sexy as fuck." He rolled a shoulder in a half-shrug, adding, "Lucky me. I'm the one who will always be taking you home."

Nodding slowly, Keefe murmured, "Yes." He flipped his hand and gave Salem's a squeeze. "You will be."

Something in Keefe settled. While it was true that, as Salem had mentioned, he didn't do wine and roses, he was honest to the point of brutality. He told it like it was, and he didn't seem to care about consequences.

However, everything he'd said and done had been angling to take care of Keefe.

I don't need wine and roses when I have his care.

Ignoring those around him, Keefe focused on his meal and his companion. The food was delicious, and the service friendly, even murmuring their congratulations. The view outside was just as spectacular as Salem had mentioned. Keefe soon wondered how the river looked in the daylight from the roof, and he mentioned that to Salem.

Salem shrugged. "I don't know. I've never been on the roof."

"You haven't?" Keefe questioned, surprise filling him. Then he hummed. "Right. Krispin's sanctuary."

"Exactly," Salem confirmed. Stabbing a sausage link, he added, "It's not quite noon. Should we check it out before checking in with our superiors?"

Keefe nodded, understanding why Salem was speaking carefully. A paranormal had to be careful what they said while within earshot of humans. Grabbing his coffee, Keefe hurried to finish his meal faster.

Taking the elevator to the roof, Keefe felt anticipation thrum through him.

Salem must have picked up on his nerves, for he threaded his fingers through Keefe's, drawing his attention. "Is everything okay?"

Keefe squeezed Salem's hand, appreciating that he seemed to be coming more and more comfortable with physical contact. "Yes. Just never felt the sun on my flesh before."

Giving him a small smile, Salem rumbled, "Well, I'm glad I get to share this with you then."

Before Keefe could reply, the elevator opened to the rooftop garden. He hesitated only an instant before taking that first step into the sun. Inhaling deeply, he relished the wonderful scent of flowers, trees, and other greenery. Keefe could admit that it looked so much prettier in the sunshine — more vibrant, somehow.

Keefe guided Salem along the paths, seeing as he was the one familiar with the space. He pointed out where he would roost every day. Then he indicated the stone forms of Phineas and Perconz.

When Keefe spotted Clinton, the coven gardener, he received an odd look. When he shifted his focus to Salem, he cocked his head, and confusion and concern creased his features. At least, that was until Keefe was obviously close enough for Clinton to scent him.

Clinton's green eyes widened, and he grinned. "I'd heard you found your mate, Enforcer Keefe." His attention flicked back and forth between Keefe and Salem. "And with Enforcer Salem. Congratulations to you both."

They both thanked the gardener for his words before they continued on.

Finally, Keefe reached the edge of the rooftop, and he

peered over the ledge. He only glanced at the streets below for a second before staring at the river. The view was even more gorgeous than from the restaurant—white water churning through the rapids and sunlight sparkling off the surface.

Keefe inhaled deeply before letting it out on a long sigh. Leaning against a wooden trellis, he just stared for several long minutes. He finally shook himself out of the moment and looked toward Salem. Noticing the vampire's gaze was pinned on him instead of the water, he smiled at his lover.

Salem smiled back, and even his dark eyes seemed to soften.

"When was the last time you were able to slow down and just look," Keefe asked curiously.

Clicking his tongue, Salem paused a few seconds, appearing to give the question the deliberation it deserved. Finally, he admitted, "It's been a while. Normally, my downtime is an evening used to find a donor."

Tightening his hold on Salem, Keefe rumbled, "You'll never have to do that again."

Salem's smile widened. The scent of his pleasure filled the air. "I know." Then he lifted their joined hands. And continuing to hold Keefe's gaze, he nipped at his knuckle. "Now I've been blessed with my beloved, I'll definitely be figuring out how to enjoy some of that elusive downtime."

Keefe chuckled. "That's something we're probably both going to have to try to figure out."

"Together then," Salem agreed.

"Together."

After another kiss to Keefe's knuckles, Salem stated, "We should probably at least check in. I know it's pretty standard for a newly mated couple to be given several days off to cement their bond, but"—he frowned and shook his head—"during these rough times, I'm not certain we'll get it."

Nodding, Keefe turned so they could head back to the elevator. "I never did hear how your patrols went," he admitted with a chuckle. "Too busy being distracted."

Salem snorted his amusement. "Not sorry."

"Me either," Keefe admitted.

"Well, I didn't take the time for a full debrief from Basques, but I did recognize at least one guy," Salem told him. "I managed to catch up with him while Merlick ran down one of his friends and Pierce snagged the other."

"Yeah?" They reached the elevator, and Keefe hit the down button. "What happened?"

"I can't say what happened with the other guys, but I learned from Marc that due to them seeing me, their plans have been put on hold." As they stepped into the elevator, Salem added, "As it turns out, Fiona's companion is one of the leaders, so I bet she's neck-deep in the priests. They also murdered the pair of guys who approached me in the bar. Used them as an example of what happens when they don't recognize a monster when they see one." Shaking his head, he told him, "Now, I've no love lost for any of those assholes, but that cold-bloodedness ramps up the danger factor for these guys."

"Why would Marc share all that with you?" Keefe asked curiously. The elevator ride lasted just long enough for him to admit, "If I were questioning someone, I can't imagine I'd think to ask about that."

Salem stepped out of the elevator onto the thirteenth floor first. "I scanned his mind for how Marc stumbled upon vampires and what he was doing with the priests."

Keefe froze. Salem kept walking, the movement tugging him forward a step before his vampire noticed and paused. The door tapping into Keefe got him moving again.

"Keefe?" Salem cocked his head for an instant. Then his

dark eyes narrowed. "Not upset about that, are you? I confirmed he was an enemy first."

Shoving his unease deep down, Keefe cleared his throat. At the same time, he rubbed the back of his neck. "I—" He couldn't lie to his mate. Hell, the man was a vampire, so he would be able to scent it even if he tried. Knowing he needed to be honest, Keefe admitted, "The idea of trancing someone still makes me uncomfortable."

Salem's jaw tightened a smidge before he dipped his chin in a sharp nod. "Noted." Then his eyes narrowed as he pinned Keefe with a hard stare. *What about this gift?*

Keefe gasped upon hearing Salem speak directly into his mind. He'd completely forgotten that when a vampire bonded with their fated mate, they were blessed with the ability to speak telepathically.

Blessed, that was the key part of his thought.

Forcing his pulse to even, at least a little, Keefe tried to respond in kind. *It will take some getting used to.* Noticing the way Salem's eyes widened just a little, he figured he'd managed to pull it off. *You are my mate, the other half of my soul. Every coming together has a bump or two along the way.*

Nodding slowly, Salem reached out and took Keefe's hand again.

So they do.

Keefe didn't bother responding as they made their way toward the offices to see who was around.

Chapter Nine

Salem knew that Keefe was uncomfortable with his ability to enter and manipulate a human's mind. Still, he was a vampire. It was part of their nature. He couldn't change it, even if he'd wanted to, and in truth, he didn't.

I am who I am.

With that, however, Salem did feel the nagging, insistent desire to please his beloved. That meant he would need to learn to keep his mouth shut about it. He wouldn't lie, but he wouldn't purposefully bring it up, either.

Just like the inner circle had recommended.

With how relaxing the morning had been, Salem would admit that he'd forgotten that tidbit of advice. He would make certain it didn't happen again.

Having fortified that in his mind, Salem led the way into the suite set up as offices for Krispin, Ridger, and Basques, as well as a large conference room. He spotted the open conference room door, so he headed in that direction first. Few people had access to the thirteenth floor, since their leader's private residences were on it, too. Salem's security clearance had been returned to him as soon as he'd returned to the building, allowing him to come and go as needed.

"Good morning, Salem," Krispin greeted as they entered the conference room. Rising to his feet, he grinned at them. "And I will assume this is Keefe's human form, considering you're holding his hand." He took several steps toward them, meeting them halfway to the lounging area. "Congratulations to you both."

That started several rounds of *thank yous* and *congratulations* with the others in the room—the rest of the inner circle, a couple of enforcers, and trackers. Wash, Vermidian, and Dennis rounded out the gargoyles.

"Looking good there, Keefe," Dennis claimed, patting him on the upper arm. "As my lovely Mandy would say, watch out, Salem. You'll have to beat 'em off your man with a stick."

Arching one brow, Salem wasn't entirely certain what the gargoyle meant. Guessing it was some kind of compliment to Keefe's human form, he gamely replied, "Then I will endeavor to always have a stick handy."

Dennis tipped his head back and laughed. "You do that, buddy."

Buddy. Salem couldn't remember the last time someone had called him that.

Not bothering to draw attention to it, Salem turned toward the sideboard. "Can I get you a drink, Keefe? There's probably most choices here."

"Just a cup of coffee would be fine, thanks," Keefe replied before settling on a sofa near Vermidian. "Elder, is there any way I can assist?"

Salem listened to the elder's reply of, "Not currently, Keefe. Now it's a waiting game as we gather more information."

Turning with a coffee for each of them, Salem saw Keefe's nod even as he scowled. "What information do we need to gather? And how?"

Vermidian hesitated before chuckling. "Well, Ninevah is digging in a virtual way. On his computer."

Salem fought back a smirk upon seeing Keefe's disgusted look. While they hadn't chatted a whole lot the evening before—he'd been too worn out from a mix of long hours awake, injury and healing, followed by several rounds of vigorous sex—Salem had learned that Keefe was not a fan of computers. His phone was about the only concession he made in that regard, and even that one he used only because he had to.

My beloved doesn't even text. Go figure.

Salem handed over a cup of coffee, which Keefe appeared grateful for. Then he settled on the sofa beside him and rested his free hand on his beloved's thigh. He took a sip of his drink before perching his mug on the armrest.

"So there's nothing I can help with?" Keefe sounded particularly put out.

Vermidian sighed before telling him, "Well, Krispin's people captured a total of six priests last night. The five that could be tranced have already been stripped of what information they have."

Salem felt Keefe's leg muscles tighten beneath him, and a hint of unease entered his scent. Either Vermidian didn't notice or he decided to ignore it.

"The sixth person was a woman, and she was interrogated the old fashion way," Vermidian told them. "The vampires and Phineas are damn certain they managed to pry everything out of her." The elder hesitated before adding, "Of the five who could be touched mentally, three were new arrivals. They've not taken a life yet, so their memories were altered, and Krispin's people are taking them to different locations to begin new lives." Vermidian's features hardened when he finished, "The other two have taken many lives and have trained others how to do the same. They were executed already as was the woman who couldn't be tranced."

Keefe nodded slowly. "I see."

Salem had no idea how to interpret those softly spoken words. They sounded as if they contained a wealth of thoughtfulness within them. Even as Salem contemplated asking Keefe for his thoughts, he knew he wouldn't.

If his beloved wished to open up, there would be a much better time and place for it.

I can wait.

"There is something you guys can do," Krispin stated,

drawing their attention.

"Anything, Master," Salem quickly answered.

Krispin smirked at him. "You could take this time to strengthen your bond. Do things together. Relax." He grinned and winked. "Hell, go on a date. I bet there are all sorts of things Keefe hasn't had the opportunity to try." Waving his hand toward Salem's gargoyle, Krispin suggested, "Now that Keefe has a human form, you could go into the city and check stuff out." His master's expression softened as he turned his attention on Wash. "Why, when Wash and I first got together, I didn't have long before I started showing, so we only got to do a few things, but I still remember that romantic carriage ride through the older sections of town."

Wash chuckled as he waggled his eyebrows. "Yes, once I convinced you to stop trying to correct the tour guide's historical facts, we had a great time."

Barking a laugh, Krispin rolled his eyes. "Oh, come on. The guy totally glossed over the real history. Dirty miners. Rampant theft. Duels to the death. It was ridiculous."

"Oh, my love," Wash rumbled, smiling as he shook his head. "You said it yourself. It was a romantic horse-drawn carriage ride. *Romantic*," he repeated. "It's his job to romanticize the town for a couple in love."

Krispin heaved an aggrieved sigh. "He could at least not make shit up. There was no school teacher saved by a sheriff from bandits who then married her. In those days, the only children here were those who helped the washer women."

"It's okay, Krispin," Wash replied. "This evening, we'll watch *You've Got Mail*, and we'll get the romance fix you need."

As Krispin growled, "Thank you," a few others chuckled.

Salem lifted one shoulder in a half-shrug. "I don't know what you all are laughing about. Tom Hanks is great in that movie. Hot, too."

Keefe snapped his attention to him, gaping. "You have a crush on him?"

Shaking his head, Salem countered. "I do not. I'm just saying he was hot in that movie."

"You're mine," Keefe snarled, pinning him with a narrow-eyed and feral stare.

Salem smiled, holding the look. "Yes, my gargoyle. I am yours." Squeezing Keefe's thigh, he added, "Just as you are mine." Once he saw that Keefe seemed appeased, he winked and asked, "So, I guess we should talk about where we want to go on our first date this afternoon."

Keefe began to answer, but he was stopped by a jaw-cracking yawn.

That was when it hit Salem. Keefe normally slept during the day. He'd already been up all night. As Salem fought his own yawn, he realized spending a few extra hours in bed sleeping didn't sound like such a bad idea.

Setting down his coffee, Salem rose to his feet. "Come on," he urged, holding out his hand. "Let's get some more rest before we decide."

Nodding, Keefe allowed Salem to help him to his feet and set aside his own half-drank cup of coffee. "I'll have my phones on the nightstand if anything comes up, Master," he told him.

Krispin just shooed at him.

Then they returned to Salem's rooms. As he closed the door behind them, he made a mental note to move Keefe's stuff out of whatever suite he'd been staying in. His beloved would no longer need it.

After removing first Keefe's clothes, then his own, Salem joined his gargoyle in the bed. Even tired, they still couldn't resist a slow make-out session culminating in a rub-off before drifting off to sleep.

Salem found exploring the city with Keefe an eye-opening experience. The things he took for granted every day—crowded sidewalks, a small local zoo, and even thrift stores—Keefe found fascinating. His gargoyle had explained that he'd read about so much online, but he'd never before had the opportunity to experience it.

With that thought in mind, Salem and Keefe spent most of the afternoon just walking around the city. He had trouble keeping his wits about him because he was too distracted watching Keefe's reactions.

The zoo had definitely been the highlight of the day. It wasn't a large one, by any means. It probably boasted only a couple of dozen animals—from flamingos to red fox to chimpanzees. There was a small bird sanctuary with a half dozen different unique species, and they'd spotted sea otters, snakes, and tortoises. There was even a petting zoo.

For some reason, Keefe found the guinea pig run absolutely hilarious. In the petting zoo area, a wooden chute had been set up to a door to the indoor guinea pig enclosure. Weather permitting, they would open the door and have the guinea pigs run the twenty feet of trough-line and into an outdoor enclosure.

"Gods, look at how fast their little legs move," Keefe had whispered into Salem's ear. "And they're all different colors." After another moment of watching several more pigs run the course to their outside home, Keefe had murmured, "Did you know that they're not related to pigs, were originally from South America raised as a meat source, and don't happen naturally in the wild? Fascinating."

"And I hear they make great pets," Salem had said back, just as softly. "Should we find a local pet store that carries them? I can get you one."

Keefe had straightened, peering at him with alarm etched over his face. "Absolutely not." He shook his head quickly.

"No pets."

Chuckling, Salem had felt a great wealth of relief. As he'd guided Keefe away from the exhibit, he'd commented, "No children and no pets. Agreed."

His beloved had practically sagged in relief against him before catching himself and straightening.

Later that evening in one of the area's nicer restaurants, the back of Salem's neck prickled. His instincts were screaming at him that someone was watching them. He attempted to pinpoint where the watcher could be, but he couldn't find anything out of place.

Keefe quickly caught on to his unease, for he reached across the dinner table and rested his hand over Salem's own. Leaning as if to whisper something romantic, he asked, "What are you feeling?"

"The hairs on the back of my head are standing on end," Salem admitted, leaning close to Keefe. "I feel as if someone is watching us. What about you?"

For just an instant, Keefe grimaced, but it was gone just as quickly. Instead, a smile that Salem easily pinned as fake—although he didn't think most others would notice—crossed Keefe's features. "I'm sorry to say, I've felt as if people have been staring all day. I'm not used to crowds, so I couldn't tell you unless I actually caught someone's eye."

"Damn," Salem grumbled. "I hadn't thought of that. I'm sorry."

Shaking his head, Keefe reminded, "You wouldn't have known." He picked up his wine glass and took a sip. Raising his voice to normal volume, he stated, "I really think I'm much too full for dessert." With a wink, Keefe added, "Unless you want to take it *to go* so I can eat it off of you."

Salem understood exactly what Keefe was doing—getting them out of there swiftly. If priests were about, there was no telling how many of them were around. Trouble could come from any direction.

"I do like the way you think," Salem replied with a sultry smile of his own. Then he lifted his hand, catching the waitress's attention. "Check, please, and will you add a slice of the strawberry cheesecake to it, please? To go."

She grinned broadly at them. "I'll hurry and get that taken care of for you, sirs." Then she was gone again.

True to her word, she was back momentarily with the check. After a quick once-over, Salem handed it right back to her along with his debit card. When she returned a few minutes later, she had not only his receipt, but their *to go* bag as well.

"Have a fantastic evening," she told them.

Rising and grabbing the bag at the same time, Salem assured, "We will. Thank you again for the wonderful service."

The young woman blushed prettily. "It was my pleasure." Then she scurried off to continue her work.

Stepping outside, Salem mentally cursed himself. He hadn't realized how late it had grown, and darkness had fallen when they'd been eating dinner. Placing his hand on his beloved's lower back, he guided him through the parking lot to their SUV, all the while keeping his eyes open for trouble.

Salem had just clicked the fob to unlock the SUV's doors when the glass window of a car near them shattered.

"Shit," Salem snarled, ducking and pulling Keefe down with him. "Move quickly."

Keefe didn't have to be told twice. His beloved swiftly duck-walked around one car to the far side of their SUV. Salem opened the back door, and they both hopped in, quickly slamming the door behind them. Salem immediately engaged the locks before they both climbed into their seats.

As Salem fired up the SUV, he tried to spot the shooter. The gleam of streetlight flickering off a gun's barrel drew his attention to the alley between the restaurant and a closed bakery. While he wished he could go charging out there to find the bastards, his instinct to see to his beloved's safety overrode it.

Gargoyle enforcer or not, Salem couldn't put Keefe in harm's way.

Instead, he put the vehicle in gear and tore the hell out of there.

See. Mating makes you do dumb shit. I could have captured that shooter, but instead, I ran.

Just as quickly, Salem realized how stupid that thought was. He had no idea how many there were or if that had been the only shooter.

Geez, we seriously need to stop these assholes.

Just as swiftly, another stupid thought entered his mind.

Shit. I dropped the cheesecake in the parking lot.

<h1 style="text-align:center">Chapter Ten</h1>

"It's good you didn't go after them yourselves." Master Krispin glanced between Keefe and Salem. "Ninevah hacked into several traffic camera feeds. There were three in the alley where the shots were being fired from."

Salem growled from where he sat next to Keefe. "Three would have been easy to take out."

Keefe silently agreed.

Krispin obviously didn't agree, for he was shaking his head. "In that alley," he stressed. "There were three more waiting on the other side of the restaurant and another six behind the closed bakery." Lifting his hands in placation, the master continued, "It's better that you came back in one piece to tell us of the attack rather than disappearing and probably getting killed."

Rubbing his palm over Salem's thick thigh, Keefe rumbled, "I don't like it, but it's for the best." As soon as they'd hit their quarters, Keefe had pulled his shirt from his body and toed off his shoes and socks. Returning to his true form had felt oddly fantastic, and with his added height, Salem had to look up to him. Keefe took advantage and cradled his mate's jaw. "We will catch these guys, but it's going to take a little longer than we'd hoped. That's all."

Keefe would give anything to keep his mate safe, regardless of the fact that he was a big, bad, and feared fixer for the coven. He'd heard the rumors. His vampire didn't really have friends because he was so feared—not just due to his deadly abilities, but also his hold-no-prisoners attitude.

My mate is a badass, but he can still be taken down by a bullet to the brain or heart. I'll do anything I can to stop that from happening.

Does that include accepting that his trancing skill could save his life?

Shoving the disturbing thought from his mind, Keefe returned his attention to Salem when he felt his vampire jerk a single nod underneath his touch.

"We *will* catch them," Salem confirmed. He turned to peer at his master. "Permission to return to the scene with a team to search for clues."

"Granted," Krispin confirmed. Then he held up his hand, saying, "But not Keefe." When Keefe opened his mouth to counter the statement, the vampire master continued, "I understand wanting to watch your mate's back. I truly do. But you're not trained for searching in the city." Spreading his arms wide, Krispin stated, "I'm sorry, but at this point, you'd just be a liability."

Keefe felt his gut clench, and a stab slashed through his heart. What Krispin said was true, but damn did it hurt to hear. He knew nothing about how to read scent currents marred by vehicle traffic and sewer and gas lines. Besides, Keefe knew that being with Salem meant his vampire's focus was on him. That was the whole reason they'd fled the restaurant. He couldn't pinpoint who was watching and from where, and Keefe had zero ability to help.

I'll learn. But that doesn't mean I can't help another way.

With that vow in mind, Keefe rumbled, "I understand." Then he turned and focused on Salem. "You be damn careful out there. Understand?"

"I'm always careful, Keefe," Salem claimed, lifting his hand to his lips and touching a chaste kiss to his palm.

That wasn't good enough for Keefe.

Using his free hand, Keefe gripped Salem's neck. Then he tugged with the hand holding his beloved's. Satisfaction filled him when Salem didn't resist, coming to him willingly.

Keefe settled his lips on Salem's and thrust his tongue between them. Sweeping deeply, he tasted his mate, enjoying his flavor. He broke the kiss just as quickly, knowing their bonding was so new, it could oh-so-easily get out of hand.

"I'll see you soon," Keefe assured, rising to his feet.

"We have our bond," Salem reminded. "I'll keep you apprised."

Keefe dipped his chin in a swift nod, sending his mate a single word. *Good.* Then he headed toward the office door and exited.

Pausing outside, Keefe inhaled deeply, trying to get his disjointed thoughts in order. As he stood there, he heard Salem's deep rumbly voice comment, "You know Keefe gave in way too easily. Don't you?"

"Indeed," Master Krispin responded.

Smiling, Keefe started away from the office.

My mate already knows me so well.

Keefe headed to the left, striding toward Elder Vermidian's quarters. After knocking, he waited impatiently. The door was opened by Perconz.

"Keefe," Perconz greeted, sounding surprised. "Is everything okay?" His golden brow ridges furrowed as he looked beyond him. "Where's your mate? I would have thought you two would continue to be joined at the hip for another few days, at least."

"They needed him to go out on assignment," Keefe told the other gargoyle. "Is Phineas on duty with you?"

Elder Vermidian appeared at Perconz's shoulder. "Keefe, did you want to come in?" He frowned at him. "Is everything okay?"

"He's looking for Phineas," Perconz answered for him even as he swung the door wider.

"Ah." Vermidian nodded. "Due to us being on lockdown, I didn't see the point in having two guards sit around with me while Ridger isn't here." He smiled wryly. "I told him to go find something else to do but to keep his phone on him."

"Thank you, Elder," Keefe replied, dipping his head in appreciation and taking a step away. "I'll track him down."

"Wait," Vermidian called, and Keefe couldn't ignore an elder's command, so he stopped and looked at him. "Is something wrong?"

Keefe sighed and lifted his hand to rub at the back of his neck. After licking his lips, he stated, "My mate is being sent out on investigative duties." He swallowed hard and shifted from foot to foot. "I need a distraction."

Perconz barked a laugh before saying, "Oh, so you're going to collect on your debt. Make Phineas watch a documentary with you." He continued to grin as he nodded. "Good idea."

In truth, that hadn't occurred to Keefe, but he wasn't going to admit that. "Thank you," he said instead.

Even Vermidian scoffed as he shook his head. "Good luck with that." Then they moved away, and the door began to swing closed.

Keefe didn't wait. He hurried to the stairwell and took the steps three at a time to reach the next floor. After swiping his card to exit, Keefe strode swiftly to Phineas's door, hoping to find him in his suite.

To Keefe's relief, when he knocked, it only took a moment for Phineas to answer the door. His friend's brow ridges shot up, even as a smile curved his lips. "Hey, Keefe. What's up?" Just as swiftly, he sobered. "Everything all right? I heard you bonded and shit. Was spending the day with your mate. What's up?"

Fortunately, as Phineas had been talking, he'd also opened the door wider and stepped backward, silently offering him entrance. Keefe took him up on that. From the looks of things—considering the TV on pause and the beer bottle on the coffee table—the other gargoyle had been relaxing.

When the door closed behind him, Keefe turned and met

Phineas's gaze. "I need your help," he stated. "There's no one here that I'd feel safer having my back."

Even as confusion filled Phineas's dark-brown eyes, he started nodding. "Yeah, man. Name it."

"Come with me. I need a spotter."

Phineas's brow ridges furrowed, and the confusion in his scent thickened. "A spotter? What do you mean?"

Keefe explained about the attack outside the restaurant and how he couldn't accompany Salem. However, he still wanted to be able to watch his vampire's back.

"So, we do what gargoyles do best," Keefe stated, curving his lips into a hard smile. "We use the skies. Or, in this case, the rooftops."

Blowing out a breath, Phineas warned, "You know this could get us both in a lot of trouble . . . especially if someone sees us."

Shaking his head, Keefe stated confidently, "Even if someone sees us, they won't spot us enough to actually get suspicious. We've used disguises before." Scoffing, he added, "Besides, people have been writing us off as myths for centuries, and the only ones actually looking for us are the bad guys." When Phineas still hesitated, Keefe rumbled, "Please, my friend. I'll do it without you, but I'd much rather have an extra set of eyes and ears to watch my back." Then a thought occurred, and Keefe smirked. "And we'll call us even for that bet."

Phineas grinned broadly. "I'm in."

When Keefe, Vermidian, and Phineas had first moved in, they'd been given keycards that accessed everything, although they'd been warned not to go to the human floors. At the time, they hadn't even known about the hidden basement floors below the underground parking garage. Now, that overall security access card had come in handy.

After donning trench coats and hats, Keefe and Phineas headed to the basement. They'd logged out a rifle, an extra scope, and a pair of handguns, as well as several boxes of ammunition for them. Then they'd headed back upstairs.

The trickiest part had been getting to the garden elevator. They'd lucked out, as no one happened to walk through the thirteenth-floor lobby as they'd waited for the car.

As they'd reached the garden level, Keefe's phone rang. He pulled it free of its strap and groaned. Seeing Ninevah's name displayed, he truly thought they were busted.

Keefe stepped out of the elevator as he accepted the call, willing to deal with whatever came his way.

"What are you doing?"

The blunt question surprised Keefe, but he didn't stop moving toward the edge of the building. "I'm going to back up my mate, gargoyle style," he told the vampire tech guru bluntly. "I'm going to cover his back." Reaching the edge of the building, Keefe took in the buildings and swept his gaze over the complex network of streets.

"You're going the wrong way."

Frowning, Keefe cocked his head. "What?" Confusion and surprise flooded him in equal manner.

A put-upon sigh sounded through his line. "Salem and his team are checking out the alleys around the restaurant you had your date at, right? The Water's View?"

"Yes." Keefe couldn't help but ask, "How did you know where we went?"

Snorting, Ninevah revealed, "I monitor credit card activity as well as our team's movements. I know just about everything there is to know about what goes on in the coven."

"Ooookaaay." Keefe thought that was a little creepy. He exchanged a look with Phineas, who sported an expression that told him his fellow gargoyle felt the same.

"Anyway, The Water's View is in the opposite direction.

Keep your phone on. I'll guide you. I'll also make certain you don't go anywhere that'll put you on security footage."

Keefe decided to take the vampire at face value. "Okay." He turned and quickly made his way through the garden and to the other side of the building. After whipping off his coat, he draped it over his weapons before checking out the area. "Coast clear?"

While Keefe had been asking Phineas, who nodded, it was Ninevah who answered. "Yes."

Shrugging, Keefe put his phone on speaker, then attached it to his torso strap. He spread his wings and jumped. To his left, he saw Phineas do the same.

Keefe caught an air current, which lifted him upward. Dipping a wing, he adjusted his angle, then flapped. He shot forward and easily made it to the roof of the next building, where he landed.

Once again, Phineas was right beside him.

"Okay, turn forty-five degrees to your right," Ninevah instructed. "You're going to want to catch the corner building there."

Over the next several minutes, Ninevah told them where to go, and they followed. A few times, Keefe had felt an uncomfortable twist in his gut. A worrisome niggle of unease that maybe the vampire techie wasn't on the up and up.

Keefe reminded himself that Ninevah was a highly valued and trusted member of the inner circle. That had to be enough for him, too. When the chimes started ringing through the line, Keefe bobbled in mid-air before catching himself and landing on the building Ninevah had indicated.

"What is it?" Keefe demanded. He could hear Ninevah cussing a blue streak through the line, although it was obvious that he wasn't speaking to them. Louder, Keefe demanded, "Ninevah, what's going on?"

"They're being ambushed," Ninevah told them, tension

filling his voice. "I see three SUVs bearing down on them as well as six motorcycles. Shit, shit, shit."

"Where?" Keefe roared.

"Just on the other side of the next building," Ninevah stated. Then he barked, "Master Krispin, we have a problem."

Keefe exchanged a look with Phineas. Then they both took off sprinting in the general direction they'd been heading. When they reached the end of the building, they dropped to the shorter one attached to it and kept on running. The next attached building was taller, but with wings and claws, it was simple to scale that one, too.

Before they even reached the edge, the sound of suppressed gunfire filled the air. Keefe skidded to a stop at the edge and peered over the ledge. His heart surely tried to pound out of his chest.

Two of the team of six vampires lay crumpled on the ground at the mouth of the alley. The remaining four were crouched behind dumpsters, hiding from the humans who had them surrounded.

"Salem isn't one of the men down," Phineas assured. "Just try to relax."

Seeing that his friend was right, Keefe felt his pulse begin to slow once more. He knelt behind the rooftop's ledge and set up the rifle on the small tripod. Then he peered through the scope.

To his left, Keefe noted Phineas move several paces away from him with his handgun in his palm.

Keefe dismissed not only his buddy, knowing his friend would do everything he could to keep him safe, but the sound of Ninevah explaining the situation to Krispin.

Peering through the scope, Keefe found his first target and fired. He kept firing . . . until pain exploded through his shoulder, knocking him back to sprawl across the roof. After a shake of his head and a glance at the wound, Keefe crawled back into position, lifted his rifle, and started again.

91

Chapter Eleven

"Where the fuck did they come from?" Salem snarled, glaring at Connor, who was hiding behind the dumpster with him.

"Hell if I know," Connor replied around a grumble. "Why didn't Ninevah warn us?" Scowling, he tried to glance around the metal canister. When a spray of bullets greeted him, Connor quickly yanked his head back to safety. "Shit. I can't tell if Petre and Kyle can survive those wounds."

"Ninevah can't keep eyes on every street," Salem stated, glaring at nothing. "We should have been paying more attention. The roaring vehicle engines were a dead giveaway."

What the hell was I thinking?

Oh, that's right. I was worried about my beloved.

Gods, I shouldn't be out here until our bond is secure and we're more comfortable with each other.

Salem knew that other bonded vampires still managed to do their jobs, so they obviously had to know something he didn't.

I'm gonna have to talk to Basques about that.

Thinking of him, Salem yanked out his phone and called his boss.

"I know, Salem. Ninevah's on the line with Krispin," Basques stated by way of greeting. "Sit-rep."

"Unknown number of priests got the jump on us. Petre and Kyle are down. I don't know if it's permanent," Salem rattled off, glad to hear their predicament was already known. "I'm pinned behind a dumpster with Connor. DeWalt and Livvie are behind another dumpster. We can't even pop up to get a shot off or get a lay of the land without bullets peppering us."

"Son of a bitch," Basques snarled. "Damn it. Sit tight. We have four teams screaming your way, but it'll be a few minutes. We—"

The crack of a high-powered rifle report echoed through the air, followed by the sound of a human's scream. The rifle shot came again . . . and again. By the fourth blast, Salem's ears were beginning to ring.

"Holy fucking hell!" Connor yelled, probably because his ears were also affected. "What the hell is going on?"

Salem chanced a peek around his corner of the canister. To his surprise, several humans had fallen, and they were now ducking behind their vehicles. Many of them had switched the direction of where they were pointing, although Salem spotted a few nervously glancing back and forth.

"We have an angel," Salem mumbled just as one of the remaining watchers spotted him peeking and took a shot. In the next instant, that human lay sprawled on the ground, his forehead half-gone. "Well, fuck me."

"Salem!"

Realizing the cry had come from his phone, Salem lifted it back to his ear. Through the buzzing, he managed to make out Basques asking what the fuck was going on.

"From the looks of things, there's a sniper or two on a nearby rooftop, and they're taking out the priests," Salem told his boss.

"Can you see who?" Basques demanded. "We don't have anyone out—" He paused, then asked, "What?"

Frowning, Salem admitted, "No, we have no visibility."

"Well, damn. I guess he is one of ours," Basques told him right before he let out a noise between a laugh and a scoff.

Confused, Salem demanded, "What's going on? Who is it?"

"Ninevah says it's Keefe and Phineas," Basques revealed. "Keefe has the rifle. Phineas is using a handgun, covering him. They're on the roof."

Salem froze. His beloved was on the roof. Why the hell would he be on the roof?

Then Salem recalled his unease from earlier in the evening . . . how he'd known his beloved had given in far too easily. "Son of a bitch," he whispered. Anger mixed with a deep well of pride within him at his gargoyle's antics, and he wasn't really sure which would win. "Gods, he'd better stay safe."

Just then, Salem heard the faintest cry of Keefe's name, and things became deadly quiet.

Salem felt as if his heart stopped for a second. He waited a second, ignoring Basques's hollering in favor of trying to hear . . . anything. The ringing in his ears didn't help.

Then, just as suddenly, that high-powered rifle report sounded through the air once more. His breath left him in a whoosh, and he crumpled on the ground. He took a few quick breaths before managing to get himself under control.

Finally, Salem realized what he should have done before. He reached out. *Keefe, Ninevah says that's you up there. Is that right?*

There was the slightest pause between one shot and the next. *Yes. I'm up here. Someone had to watch your back. We'd already been shot at once this evening. What the hell were you thinking only taking a team of six?*

Salem couldn't help himself. He had to smile upon hearing Keefe's disgruntlement, even through his mental voice.

I love you, too, handsome.

He sent the mental thought even before he'd made the conscious decision to do it. Well, shit, he thought, keeping that particular one to himself. He didn't know when he'd gone and done that. Hell, he'd known the gargoyle less than forty-eight hours. Didn't that make it too soon?

Once again, there was a slight hitch between one round and the next. *Good. I love you, too, and I know what you're thinking, mister badass fixer. It's too soon, but here's something you forgot. We're paranormals. We do everything fast.*

Salem actually barked a laugh out loud, which drew a disbelieving look from Connor. Shaking his head, he couldn't help but tease his beloved right back. *We don't do everything fast, my handsome gargoyle. In fact, I remember the hours of lovemaking we enjoyed not too long ago. It wounds me that you can forget so quickly.*

Keefe's warm chuckles flooded his mind.

He really liked that sound.

Fyi. I'm just about out of ammo. How many of these damn motherfuckers are going to come crawling out of the woodwork, and where is your damn backup?

They should be here any second.

At least, Salem assumed that was true. How long had it been?

Slow your shots. Keep them behind their vehicles as best you can. We'll be fine.

Got it. Then the shots slowed, telling Salem that Keefe obeyed. The patter of a smaller caliber weapon sounded a bit more often, so he knew Phineas remained active up there.

"Salem, we have movement at the other end of the alley," Connor claimed, drawing his attention.

Scowling, Salem peered away from the bullets continued to erupt. He kept in the shadows and crept toward the other end of the alley, his own weapon in hand. They'd originally fled in that direction, but the appearance of a half-dozen guys on motorcycles had cut them off, forcing their retreat into the alley.

Salem knew the only reason those guys hadn't chased after them was because they might have gotten hit in the cross-fire from their own men. Now, that must not have been a concern. Salem spotted two forms trying to sneak toward them.

Yeah. No.

Lifting his nine-millimeter, Salem aimed and fired . . . twice. Both men dropped like stones.

As much as Salem preferred using stealth and his talons when fighting priests, they had to be prepared — hence, guns.

"DeWalt? Livvie?" Salem called. "Report."

"We're fine so far," Livvie hollered back, her voice filled with annoyance. "What the hell is going on? Is our back-up out there stopping them?"

"In a manner of speaking," Salem replied, unable to help his grin. "My beloved didn't like how small our team was, so he came to watch over us."

Connor curled his lip. "He was a little late."

"Oh, fuck you, Connor," DeWalt snapped angrily. "Fuck you and the self-righteous steed you rode in on. None of us were prepared for this, and that's our mistake. Without Salem's beloved covering us, we would all be dead."

"Congrats, Salem!" Livvie offered.

"Thanks."

Salem frowned Connor's way, who appeared to be pouting. He hadn't worked with the vampire in nearly six months, but he didn't remember him being so whiny. Salem made a mental note to keep an eye on the guy.

Just as Salem heard Basques's voice through the line telling him that their back-up had arrived, he heard another ringtone. He paused, confused as he listened to a second ring. At the sound of the third, realization struck.

My burner phone.

Scrambling with his vest, Salem yanked it out and accepted the call. "Salem here."

"Thank god you picked up." It was Marc. "I was worried. The priests hit one of your teams this evening. I'm so sorry I didn't warn you. I didn't know. I would have told you if I'd known." Before Salem could figure out how to assure the clearly upset human that it was fine, Marc hurried on to say,

"But I just learned that it's actually a decoy. They're hitting those guys to lure out your fighters. Then a smaller group is going to torch your guys' hotel."

"Oh, fuck," Salem hissed. "Do you know a time?"

Marc's voice sounded strained. "Uh, now." He sounded totally forlorn. "I'm really sorry, Salem. My phone died, and I didn't notice. I just got enough juice in it to get my messages, and well—"

"No, I get it." Salem knew he couldn't stay on the phone to soothe the human's concerns. "I've gotta go. We need to plan. I'll call you in a bit."

Then Salem hung up, but he didn't miss Marc's cry of, "I'm sorry and good luck!"

Lifting his other phone to his ear, Salem asked, "You still there, Basques?"

"I am," the head enforcer confirmed. "I'm here, too, actually. Everyone on this end is mopped up. You're free to come out this way."

"Thanks." While Salem signaled to the others that they were clear in that direction, he quickly added into the phone, "But the danger isn't over yet. This was a decoy. They're going to hit the hotel in a matter of minutes."

"Son of a—" Then Basques's line cut out.

Salem completely understood. Slowly rising to his feet, he started in the opposite direction. When he reached the far end, he noted the bodies of the two priests. Beyond that, there were two motorcycles. The other four were gone.

Shaking his head, Salem shot off a text to Ninevah and Basques. They would both need to know that four of the six bikers had fled. Then he headed back, reaching out for his beloved in the process.

I owe you one, my beloved. Salem couldn't help but smile. His pleasure at his gargoyle having his back far outweighed anything else. He felt honored he had come. *We wouldn't have made it without you.*

I'll always be there for you.

Salem froze, not liking just how weak and tired Keefe's mental voice sounded. *Baby, are you okay?* He would think about the term of endearment—something he'd never given another—some other time. *If you come down, I'll give you guys a ride home.*

Home.

He sure liked the sound of that.

I'm afraid I can't stand at the moment.

That comment caused Salem to snap his focus upward. *What do you mean?*

A bit of blood loss. Nothing a roost won't cure.

Keefe?

Salem didn't get a response. Snarling, he called his beloved's cell phone. To his relief, the line picked up. Before his gargoyle could say anything, Salem snapped into the phone, "What the hell kind of thing is that to say to me and then not answer? How badly are you injured? Where are you?"

"This is Phineas. Keefe was shot through the shoulder, Salem," a deep voice told him. "It cracked his collarbone. After Keefe dragged himself back up, he kept on firing. Now, I'm pretty sure it's fractured. He's gone into roost to heal."

Fighting back a wealth of fear, Salem roughly demanded, "Where are you?"

"Look up and to your right."

Salem obeyed, spotting a figure waving from the rooftop. "Be right there."

"I don't—"

Not caring what else Phineas had to say, Salem began sprinting toward the structure. He ignored Basques hollering his name in favor of leaping as high as possible. Using his claws and the occasional foothold of a windowsill or brick, Salem swiftly scaled the structure's wall.

Salem reached the top and flipped over the side. Glancing

around, he spotted Phineas crouched over a prone form, a rifle lying a couple of feet away. He crossed to them, his steps slowing as he realized just what Phineas had explained.

Keefe lay sprawled on the rooftop, but he was in the form of a stone statue as Salem had seen Phineas and Perconz earlier that day. There were dark streaks over his right shoulder, which looked oddly shaped compared to the left one. There was also a massive pool of blood under his right torso.

Sighing deeply, Salem sank to his knees beside his injured lover. He eased to his butt before resting his hand over Keefe's stone thigh. Oddly enough, it felt warm beneath his touch. As Salem rubbed his thumb over the male's surface, he turned his attention to Phineas.

"What happens now?"

Phineas's brow ridges furrowed. "What do you mean?"

Salem returned his focus to Keefe. "He went into roost in the middle of the night. How does that work?"

Settling beside him, Phineas explained, "We only roost at night if we've been badly injured, but we know we're in a safe place to rest." He waved his hand in Keefe's direction. "I'm not sure about resting here, but he must have trusted that you would protect him while he's vulnerable."

Nodding, Salem pledged, "No harm will come to him."

"Glad to hear it," Phineas replied softly. "Anyway, he'll stay like that until he's sufficiently healed to defend himself again." Grimacing, he stared at Keefe. "With a wound like that, could be six hours. Could be ten. It really depends on the internal damage."

Salem nodded and glanced around, taking in where he would stay for the foreseeable future. Maybe he could call someone to bring him a cushion and some blankets. Salem could really use some coffee and some more ammunition, too.

"Damn it all, Salem."

Salem heard Basques's voice before he saw him.

"What are you doing?" the head enforcer snapped as he hopped over the side of the building, having obviously scaled it just like Salem had done. "We don't have time for winner's sex. We need to—" Basques's jaw sagged open as he took in Keefe's stone form. "What the hell?"

Shit. Right. The coven.

Even as Salem felt himself torn in two directions, he knew which one would win.

"I'm sorry, Enforcer Basques," Salem replied solemnly. "I can't return now. I must stay here to watch over my beloved while he heals."

Basques immediately nodded, his nostrils flaring as he clenched his jaw. "I understand." His voice sounded thick to Salem's ears. "No way I'd leave Dloben if he were in a similar situation. No matter what." He rested a hand on Salem's shoulder and squeezed lightly. "As soon as the hotel is safe, I'll send someone with supplies for your vigil."

Salem nodded once. "Thank you . . . for understanding."

Scoffing, Basques shook his head. "Nothing to thank me for." Then he picked up the rifle. "I'll see you soon."

Phineas rose to his feet, confusion filling his features. "Wait. What's going on?"

"The priests are attacking the hotel," Salem announced solemnly. He indicated the mess below. "We were the decoys."

"Well, fuck."

To Salem's surprise, Phineas sank back on his ass.

"You're not going?" Salem questioned.

Phineas shook his head, a wry smile curving his lips. "Naw. I promised Keefe I'd watch his back." After a shrug, he added, "Besides, Vermidian has Dennis, Perconz, and the rest of the coven to keep him safe. I'm needed here tonight."

Scoffing softly, Salem smiled. "Thank you."

CHAPTER TWELVE

Keefe swam to wakefulness, the hold of roost slowly releasing him. He almost wished it hadn't. Pain unlike anything he'd felt in quite some time pulsed through his shoulder.

Oh, wait. Yes. Yes, I have experienced pain worse than this recently.

Most had sucked big hairy donkey balls.

So why do I hurt now?

Just that fast, it all came back to Keefe—saving his mate only to end up damn near being forced into roost due to injury.

Gods. I can't believe I revealed the secrets of healing roost to a coven of vampires.

The fact that a gargoyle could heal from damn near anything—yes, even a bullet to the head—was a closely guarded secret. Hell, even most of the clutch chieftains didn't know it. After so many centuries where it wasn't shared with anyone but a select few—the elders and their closest enforcers, mainly—the secret had almost died out.

Until me.

"You know, if you don't want anyone to know, all you have to do is say so."

Hearing Salem's soft, deep rumble sent a rush through Keefe's system. That rush also helped ease some of his pain. He realized just as suddenly that it could also be the fact that Salem was petting one of his wings.

Gods, that feels nice.

Someone else chuckled, pulling Keefe from his happy half-dreams. He forced himself to pry open an eyelid and realized Elder Vermidian, Phineas, and Enforcer Basques were all in the room, too. Concern rode him hard when he realized he didn't recognize where he was, either, and had no idea how he'd gotten there.

"We carried you here. You're in the coven's infirmary," Elder Vermidian answered his most urgent needs. He smiled kindly. "While I wish you would have shared your plans with me, you did save your mate as well as me and almost a hundred vampires with your impetuous act."

Confusion flooded Keefe. "But . . . there were only four," he managed to croak out.

Salem immediately grabbed a cup with a straw, which he brought to Keefe's lips. "Drink a bit. You've been roosting for nearly twelve hours."

Twelve hours. Fuck.

"Damn near gave me a heart attack," Salem grumbled, frowning at him. Then his dark features softened, and he threaded his fingers through Keefe's hair. "Thank you, my beloved. Thank you so much." His smile definitely held a loving cast, making Keefe nearly melt into the bed with happiness, but his mate's words confused him. "Without you, our coven would have been lost."

Keefe frowned even as he lifted a shaky hand to grip Salem's wrist. "I don't understand," he whispered.

Salem licked his lips and glanced away. Meeting his gaze once more, he asked, "Do you remember me telling you about Marc? The priest who I tranced for information?"

Nodding, Keefe mumbled, "The one who recalled the execution of two priests because they invited you into the group?"

"Yeah. Him," Salem confirmed. "Uh . . . I actually changed his memories and sent him back into the group as an informant."

"Oh." Keefe tried to make sense of that. "How?"

Salem shrugged. "I just twisted a few of his memories in regards to how he'd learned about vampires. Changed his loyalty to his buddy to awe of how a bond could be, I suppose." He swallowed hard enough for his Adam's apple to bob. "Anyway, after you'd saved us, he called me to warn me that the attack on our patrol was a decoy to draw out our enforcers and guards. The real attack was to the coven hotel at the same time." Scoffing, Salem added, "If you hadn't gone with your gut to watch over me, I'd be dead, and Marc wouldn't have reached me, and the warning would never have reached my coven."

Keefe's mind scrambled to connect that explanation. Blinking quickly, he whispered, "Using that logic, if you hadn't tranced Marc, hadn't altered his memories, your coven would have been wiped out . . . as would me and my elder." Scoffing softly, he finally had to admit, "Guess we all have our abilities for a reason."

Clearing his throat, Salem nodded. "Guess so." He picked up Keefe's hand and pressed a kiss to his palm before softly repeating, "Guess so."

After a few seconds of silence, Basques cut in, "Due to Marc's warning, we managed to capture just about every priest sent at us." His broad grin appeared feral. "And that includes Erick and Fiona." A pleased-sounding growl escaped the head enforcer. "I'm letting them cool their heels for a while before talking to them, but most of the others have already been processed and dealt with."

Relief flooded Keefe upon realizing safety could be soon at hand. "I'm glad," he mumbled roughly.

"So, there are a very select few who know about the gargoyle roost secret," Basques reassured, smiling warmly at him. "And I'll have all of us sworn to secrecy."

"Only on life and death do we pass it along," Vermidian

explained. "For anyone to know that a gargoyle can heal from a bullet to the brain or heart, well . . . then they'd just stand over the gargoyle and slice off their head after putting them down."

"Understood," Basques confirmed. Then he grinned widely. "You know, the fact that you all can do that is actually reassuring to myself and my buddies. We're all bonded to one of your kind."

Relief flooded Keefe even as he smiled. "Thank you."

Basques dipped his chin in a nod, then excused himself and headed out.

"I am so very pleased to have one with instincts such as yours to watch my back," Elder Vermidian stated, resting his hand on Keefe's upper arm. "Rest and heal, my friend."

"Thank you, Vermidian," Keefe replied humbly.

After the elder had turned away, Phineas approached. He scowled at Keefe and shook his head. "Damn it, man. No more of that shit until I've found my own mate," he demanded with a growl. "How am I to watch your ass if I'm stuck in roost half the time?"

Keefe found himself chuckling softly upon hearing Phineas's whining. "I'll remember that." Then he smirked and added, "At least you got out of watching that documentary."

Phineas snorted, moving his hands to his hips. "Damn skippy." Turning away, he pointed at Salem. "You watch out for my buddy there, or we'll have words."

Before Keefe could manage a growl of warning, Salem nodded solemnly. "You have my vow. Always will I watch over my beloved."

"Good." Then Phineas stalked out of the room.

Salem turned back to eye Keefe. He offered him the water straw once more, and he gratefully drank. After setting it on the nightstand, to Keefe's surprise and pleasure, Salem crawled onto the bed beside him and curled around his uninjured side.

"Sleep a bit more," Salem urged, nuzzling his temple with his nose. "I have a surprise for you when you feel better."

It'd taken another twenty-four hours of healing, but Keefe was finally able to accept his surprise. He hadn't expected it when it involved driving into the forested mountains north of the city.

Salem parked the SUV in a turnout. Then he'd grabbed a blanket and bag from the back before guiding him down a narrow footpath.

It wasn't the meadow that opened before them that caused Keefe to gasp. Instead, it was the telescope. The large, very high-end model was already pointed at the sky, and Keefe fought against the shiver of anticipation he felt at getting the opportunity to stare through it.

Salem must have seen it anyway. He pecked his lips before laughing and waving toward it. "Go on, my beloved. Enjoy yourself while I set up our picnic."

Unable to resist such a sweet invitation, Keefe rushed toward the promised view of the celestial bodies. Before he peered into the eyepiece, he met Salem's gaze. "I love you."

Salem gave him that small intimate smile that Keefe had come to love so much. "I love you, too, my gargoyle."

About the Author

Charlie started writing fantasy when she was eight, and after stumbling onto her first erotic romance at age nineteen, she realized her true calling. She now focuses on writing gay erotic romance, normally of the paranormal variety, with heroes of all kinds. With the help and support of her husband, Charlie finally fulfilled one of her life-long goals . . . move to acreage with her horses. You can often find her curled up with her laptop and a cup of tea or glass of wine, creating her next adventure. Charlie enjoys exploring the mountains of her new Oregon home on horseback, 4-wheeler, or motorcycle.

She can be reached at ch.richards2010@yahoo.com

Or visit her at www.charlie-richards.com.